COUNT KARLSTEIN

Philip Pullman

Decorative illustrations by Diana Bryan

A Dell Yearling Book

Published by
Dell Yearling
an imprint of
Random House Children's Books
a division of Random House, Inc.
1540 Broadway
New York, New York 10036

Originally published in a different form in Great Britain in 1982 by
Chatto & Windus Ltd.

Visit us on the Web! www.randomhouse.com/kids

**Educators and librarians, for a variety of teaching tools,
visit us at www.randomhouse.com/teachers**

ISBN: 0-375-80348-3

Reprinted by arrangement with Alfred A. Knopf,
a division of Random House, Inc.

Printed in the United States of America

First Dell Yearling edition December 2001

10 9 8 7 6 5

CWO

To Jamie, yet once more

CAST OF CHARACTERS

Peter Kelmar

Hildi Kelmar

Miss Charlotte

Miss Lucy

Meister Haifisch

Frau Muller

Count Heinrich Karlstein

Frau (Ma) Kelmar

Sergeant Snitsch

Constable Winkelburg

Herr Arturo Snivelwurst

Doctor Cadaverezzi

Max Grindoff

Eliza

Herr Woodenkopf

Miss Augusta Davenport

Zamiel the Demon Huntsman

CONTENTS

THE JOLLY HUNTSMAN

PART ONE

Hildi

ONE

Peter crouched over the fire, stirring the embers so that the sparks swarmed up like imps on the rocky walls of hell. Behind him, his shadow shook and flared across the wall and half the ceiling of our little bedroom, and the cracks between the floorboards shone like golden rivers in the darkness.

"Listen," he said. "Zamiel!"

And with a delicious shiver I pulled my eiderdown over me and lay on the rug with my face pressed to the floor to hear the voices from the parlor below....

We lived in the tavern in Karlstein village, with our Ma, who was the landlady. A quiet enough place, though there was usually a stranger or two passing through, and the company in the tavern parlor was as good as any in the mountains—especially on a winter's night, when their pipes were going and their glasses full and there was a good story to be told.

Peter and I each had our favorites: stories of hunting for him and tales of terror for me. The best of all were

3

those about Zamiel, the Prince of the Mountains, the Demon Huntsman. There was usually a bargain in the tale, and a chase, and bloody revenge, and a frenzied victim running in terror through the snow, pursued by the Wild Hunt—great hounds with slavering jaws and luminous eyes, black horses ridden by grinning skeletons and, at the head of it all, the Demon himself, swathed in impenetrable darkness, with eyes of raging fire. Even our Ma (we'd see through the cracks in the floorboards) would pause in her work and lean her plump elbows on the counter and stare with wide eyes as the latest tale unfolded.

But none of the customers below ever came so close to Zamiel as Peter and I did, and I came closest of all: I was in the very room when he came for his victim, and I'll never forget what I saw if I live till the year 1900.

It all began on a gray afternoon in October. The year was 1816, and I'd been working at Castle Karlstein for nearly a year. (My name is Hildi Kelmar, by the way.) There had been a heavy fall of snow; I was sitting at the parlor window with a bundle of mending in my lap, and Miss Lucy and Miss Charlotte behind me were roasting chestnuts in the fire. I was looking out at the fading light and thinking of drawing the curtains to shut out the chill when I saw a coach lumbering up the narrow road. I gazed at it in surprise, because we'd had no visitors since March; and then, as the coach turned the corner into the castle courtyard, the wheels slipped on the icy road and the coach slewed round toward the precipice.

The horses whinnied with fear and the driver nearly fell off the box as the brakes screeched and failed to grip; the coach banged against the stone gateway, and came away lighter by a great strip of paint. I jumped and cried out—and then at the last moment the wheels gripped, and the coach rolled through into the courtyard. The girls ran up beside me and watched as the coachman got down and leaned shivering against the large back wheel, and mopped his forehead before opening the door of the coach.

Out there stepped, cool as you please, a skinny old gentleman in black, who looked at the coachman as if to say, "Nerves? I advise you to have 'em cut out, my man, and braided into a whip, the better to guide these shambling nags," dusted off the flakes of snow that had had the impertinence to settle on his bony old shoulders, and made his way across the white courtyard, where the darkness was already beginning to pile up in the corners, as if driven there by the wind. Johann the footman opened the castle door and let out a great quantity of light, which leapt inside again as soon as he shut it. The coachman began to unharness the horses, with many head-shakings and gesturings to the groom, while the girls tried to guess who the visitor might be.

They were English—not Swiss at all, though they'd picked up enough of our language in the time they'd been here to sound like natives. Lucy was twelve and Charlotte was ten, and I wasn't much older myself; but I counted myself more fortunate by far, because I had a mother still alive and a brother—and no grim uncle like Count Karlstein. They had no other relatives, and since their parents had both died in a shipwreck, they had no choice but Count Karlstein or an orphanage—and if they'd known what he'd be like, they'd have chosen the orphanage without a second's pause. They'd been here a year now, poor things.

He'd been here for nine, nearly. Old Count Ludwig Karlstein, the previous count, had died without an heir, so the estate had passed to Count Heinrich Karlstein, a thin, dark man, much given to gnawing his nails, muttering to himself, and poring over works of German philosophy at midnight in his stone-walled, tapestried study. Nothing so bad in those things, of course, but he had other defects, such as a temper you'd have put down for its own sake if it'd been a dog, a vile, sarcastic tongue, and—worst of all—a kind of bright-eyed delight in being cruel, whether it was to a horse or dog or a servant—or a little niece from another country, with nowhere else to go. But there it was: he was the master.

And meanwhile, Lucy had remembered who the visitor was.

"It's the lawyer, Charlotte!" she insisted. "The old man from Geneva! He gave us that dark sweet wine and some cake while we waited for Uncle Heinrich—"

"Meister Haifisch!" said Charlotte.

"That's right. Perhaps he's come to take us away again—can he do that? D'you think he could do that, Hildi?"

"Hildi, go and find out! Go and listen! Please!" said Charlotte.

"I can't do that!" I said. "They'd throw me out for good, and then where would you be? Just wait and see, that's the best thing to do."

Lucy made a face, but she saw I was right. And as it happened, none of us had long to wait, because only a minute or so later Frau Muller the housekeeper (as surly as a goose, and with the same way of leaning at you with a long neck when she was cross) came bustling in.

"Miss Lucy and Miss Charlotte! You're to go and wash yourselves and brush your hair and come down to your Uncle Heinrich in ten minutes. And you, Kelmar, put that sewing down and get along to the drawing-room—Dettweiler fell over in the courtyard and broke her ankle, stupid girl, so you'll have to be parlormaid for the time being."

They were hustled away, and I took a candle

and hastened down to the drawing-room. Poor little Susi Dettweiler—Count Karlstein had made her cry three times yesterday, and now she breaks her ankle! My heart was thumping wildly as I went in, in case my clumsiness attracted Count Karlstein's attention. I feared he'd lash at me like a tiger.

But when I opened the door, I saw him so deep in conversation with the skinny old stranger, and the skinny old stranger paying such close attention to him, that neither of them noticed me for a moment or two. I don't know what I should have done, but I stood in the shadows, too nervous to go forward, and listened to what they were saying.

"Damn it, Haifisch," said Count Karlstein (Haifisch! Lucy was right, then: this cool old skeleton was the lawyer from Geneva), "you're not *sure?* After nine years? How much longer d'you want? Would a hundred years be sufficient? Would you be able to say then, 'Yes, Count Karlstein, we have finally established that there is no other claimant—for if there was, he must be dead by now'? Eh?"

Meister Haifisch showed no sign that Count Karlstein's tone annoyed him. He was as calm as he'd been when he'd stepped out of the coach, having missed certain death by the thickness of a wheel rim.

"You asked me to make certain, Count Karlstein," he said evenly. "Certainty without evidence, in a case like this, is worthless."

Count Karlstein snorted. "Worthless! *You're* worthless, Haifisch, if you can't do better than that. If evidence is all you want, can't you manufacture some? Eh? Make it up?"

The lawyer stood up. That was all he did; but it stopped Count Karlstein's restless prowling and finger-gnawing and sideways kicks at the great log in the fire as effectively as if a gunshot had sounded. Meister Haifisch had a presence that commanded your attention. Like an actor, he knew how to make every movement count. And his audience— both of us, one in the shadows beside the door and one scowling beside the fire—was held still, waiting for his next words.

Which were simple. "Good night, Count Karlstein," was all he said; but his voice held such a charge of contempt that it would have shamed the devil himself.

"Oh, sit down, man," said Count Karlstein irritably; and I knew he'd realized that if he wanted to tamper with the truth, Meister Haifisch wasn't the man to put a legal seal on the doing of it. "Come and sit down again. I'm out of sorts—don't mind me. Go through it again, will ye…?" And he threw himself into the carved oak chair at the other side of the fireplace, bent down to tear off a strip of bark from one of the logs in the hearth, and shredded it slowly into tiny pieces as Meister Haifisch spoke.

"The only son of old Count Ludwig Karlstein was stolen from his cradle twenty years ago. I have traced him as far as

Geneva, where a child answering to the same description was placed in a foundlings' home a short while after he disappeared. That child—if it was he—grew up and became a groom, working in the stables of the Black Bear Inn; then he joined the army—and that is the last we know. His regiment was scattered at the Battle of Bodelheim; he may have been taken prisoner, or he may be dead. And that, I repeat, is all we know."

Count Karlstein grunted and slapped his thigh in irritation.

"That's the best you can do?"

"That is the best anyone can do, Count Karlstein. There is no one in Switzerland who knows more about the affairs of the estate of Karlstein than I do; and so what I have told is the limit of human knowledge on the subject."

Was there a hint of sarcasm in his tone? Maybe, but Count Karlstein didn't hear it if there was. For he looked up then, and saw me. He sprang to his feet with an oath.

"How long have you been there, hussy?" he snarled.

"Only a moment, sir! I knocked, but you didn't hear me!"

The lawyer was watching; otherwise I think the count would have hit me. He sent me out impatiently to fetch some wine, and when I came back, I found that he and Meister Haifisch had given up all attempts at conversation and were standing at opposite ends of the room, examining the books, or the pictures, or the snow-filled darkness outside the window.

I served them the wine, and then the girls came in; Meister Haifisch bent and shook their hands, and asked them how they were; and a warmth came into his expression. He looked as dry as dust and no more kindly than a silver ink-pot, but he was as polite and attentive to those two little girls as if they'd been the Duchess of Savoy and her twin sister. Lucy and Charlotte blossomed, and sat on the sofa at either side of him, sipping their wine and talking with all the elegance in the world, while their uncle prowled, gnawing his fingers, around the edges of the room and said nothing.

Presently Meister Haifisch stood up and bowed to the girls, excusing himself, as it was time to dress for dinner; and while I cleared away the glasses, Count Karlstein came and stood by the fire again and said to them:

"Lucy, Charlotte—how long have you been here now? A year, is it?"

"Almost, Uncle Heinrich," said Lucy.

The count looked down. Then abruptly he said, "How would you like a holiday?"

Both the girls looked startled for a moment, then nodded vigorously.

"We'd love it," said Lucy.

"Leaving tomorrow afternoon," he said, beaming, trying to be genial. "Just a few days, mind."

"Anything!" said Charlotte, eagerly.

"Where would we be going?" said Lucy.

"To my hunting lodge," said Count Karlstein.

Their faces dropped involuntarily—but only for a second, and then they recovered. He didn't notice.

"That would be very pleasant, Uncle Heinrich," said Lucy.

"Thank you very much," said Charlotte, trying as hard as she could to keep the disappointment out of her voice.

"Good, good, that's settled then," said the count, and dismissed them briskly, settling down at his desk and scribbling at some papers. I followed the girls out.

They were neither of them keen on hunting; and if you don't like hunting, where's the fun in staying at a hunting lodge? Deep in the middle of the forest, all set about with pine trees...Set about with wolves, too, and bears and wild boars. What would the girls do there but struggle through the deep snow and watch Count Karlstein hack the life out of some poor deer his bullets had brought twitching to the ground? What would they do in the evening but sit wrapped in furs beside the skimpy fire and watch Count Karlstein getting drunk with his chief huntsman? A fine holiday they'd have!

And then I realized something that brought a little chill

to my heart. Today was Wednesday; they were leaving tomorrow, Thursday, and staying, said the count, for a few days...which meant that they'd be at the hunting lodge on All Souls' Eve, Friday night—the very night when Zamiel the Demon Huntsman was said to ride through the forests, driving every living thing before him. Scorched hoofprints were found after his passing, they said, and animals dead of terror, with no mark upon them....

But I couldn't tell Charlotte and Lucy that. There're things best kept quiet, for fear of making them worse. So I said nothing—for the moment.

THE HUNTING LODGE

TWO

There was one person who would have enjoyed Count Karlstein's hunting lodge, and that was my brother, Peter. He was eighteen now, a fine shot, a keen hunter, and he knew the forests as well as anyone alive. Too well, perhaps; for he knew where the finest game was to be had—and he had it, and was arrested for poaching. Poaching! In old Count Ludwig's day they'd have been more indulgent—but they managed the forests better then, and game was more plentiful. At any rate, Peter was under lock and key at the police station and my poor mother was nearly frantic with worry. I wasn't; Peter was cheerful and tough, and a few days on bread and water wouldn't hurt him. But the worst thing was, he'd lose his chance of entering the shooting contest—and he'd set his heart on that for years.

This was no ordinary shooting contest. For one thing, it wasn't held regularly every year or even every five years; it was held only when the Chief Ranger of the Forest retired. And, of course, there was no ordinary prize: a few gold coins and a scroll and a medal pinned on by the Mayor—but you'd get all that and more if you won any of a dozen shooting contests up and down the valleys. No, the prize here was nothing less than the Rangership itself. The winner of the contest had the right to take charge of every living thing in the forest, whether it grew in the ground, ran over it, or flew through the air above it. And Peter had set his heart on trying for it; and now he was in jail. There wouldn't be another shooting contest for years and years, maybe. And poor Ma, at the Jolly Huntsman, was in despair—especially as the place was filling up with men and muskets from far and wide.

I begged Frau Muller for an hour or two and went down to the village to give her a hand.

And found—sitting at the kitchen table, grinning all over his silly face and digging his great fingers into a pigeon pie—no less a criminal than my poaching brother!

"Peter! What are you doing? Have they let you out?"

"Not likely," he said, stuffing another handful of pie into his face. "I escaped!"

"What!"

"I pinched the key from Constable Winkelburg's belt and got out," he said. "You should have seen Ma's face!"

I saw it then, as she came in with a tray of dirty glasses. I'd never seen anyone look so unhappy, poor soul—anxious and jumpy, as if all the policemen in Switzerland were galloping toward her at this very minute, whiskers bristling, ready to bear her off and hang her as an accomplice. And Peter just sat there feeding himself, looking as pleased as a dog with a new trick. Great smirking lump.

He couldn't understand for the life of him why we were cross.

"They'll never bother with me," he said defensively.

"'Course they will!" said Ma. "You're a wanted man, now, my lad! There'll be a price on your head and a poster on the wall of the police station. You'll be an outlaw—you'll have to flee the country! If only you'd waited there for another week—"

"And missed the shooting contest, aye," he said. "Sit there like a blooming pansy in a pot and listen to 'em shooting—not likely. I'll get out and take me chance. Anyway, like I said, they'll be too busy to bother with me. There's a famous criminal on his way!"

"How do you know?" I said. I had only an hour; I was trying to make some pastry, and I pushed him away from the table.

"I listened to the sergeant," he said. "There was a message from the authorities in Geneva, and Sergeant Snitsch had to read it out to Constable Winkelburg. It's a feller called Brilliantini, an Italian. He's been in jail in Geneva, and he got out by some trick or other, and all the police forces are being warned to keep an eye open for him."

"He could be going anywhere," said Ma. "Why expect

him to turn up here? Oh, I wish you'd stayed in that cell...."

"No, Sergeant Snitsch reckons he must be heading this way, 'cause of all the money that's going to be around when the shooting contest's on. He's a swindler, see, this Brilliantini, a confidence trickster. Old Sergeant Snitsch reckons he's going to catch him and get promoted—and Constable Winkelburg's quaking with terror in case *he* has to arrest him...." Peter shouted with laughter, and I slapped him with a wet dishcloth. Everyone knew that laugh, and if they heard it in the bar, word would get around in no time and he'd be back in jail. With handcuffs on, this time, and a heavier sentence.

"What are you going to do?" I said to him. "You can't stay here."

"'Course I can!"

Ma said nothing, but just sighed deeply and went out again.

"You can't," I said. "Don't be stupid. She's worrying herself sick over you—and where are you going to hide? In the stables? In the cellar? You'd never stay in one place for long enough! You'd stick your silly face out of the window to say hello to Rudi or Hansi and blow kisses to Hannerl, and then you'd want your musket to practice with, and then you'd want to go outside just to stretch your legs and you'd forget and come back through the parlor and stop and say hello to the customers—I *know* you, Peter! You're just irresponsible!"

"And you're middle-aged," he grumbled. "Born old, you were. Nag, nag, nag…And it just shows how much you know, because shall I tell you what I'm going to do? I'm going to stay down in the cellar and do nothing for three days but clean my musket and think hard about that target. I'm going to do some exercises too, to strengthen my arms and make them even steadier. I've got me heart set on that contest, Hildi. I'm going to win it. You think I'm irresponsible.…But there's a part of me inside that can concentrate harder'n you can imagine. All still and cold, and deeper than a forest lake…And that part of me's where I shoot from. When I'm shooting for that prize, I'm going to be stiller than the mountain—you'll see. You don't know me, Hildi, you don't know me at all.…"

Of course I knew him, silly brute. But I was impressed all the same. He'd never talked to me like that before; he sounded quiet and serious, and I thought: perhaps he *can* win the contest, at that. But it wouldn't have done to say so.

"If you're going to hide in the cellar, you'd better get on down. And if I hear from Ma that you've caused her any trouble, I promise I'll go and get Sergeant Snitsch myself and give you up. *She* wouldn't do it, because she's too soft. But I won't think twice about it, I warn you."

"Yes, ma'am," was all he said; and he took his musket from the wall and went down the steps into the cellar like a choirboy going to Mass.

I finished the pastry and rolled it out and then I had to hurry back. Before I went, I told Ma what he'd said, quietly, in a corner of the parlor so as not to be overheard.

"He's a good boy," she said. "But how's he ever going to show his face at the contest? He'll be arrested as soon as he shows up…oh, dear.…" She was going to cry, so I kissed her swiftly and left. Another party of guests entered as I did so—that'd give her something to do. I'd never seen the village so full.

I stopped outside the police station on the way back, because I saw Sergeant Snitsch nailing up a poster outside and I couldn't help wondering if they were offering a reward for Peter already. They weren't—but the poster bore out the truth of what he'd told us in the kitchen.

ATTENTION!

All citizens are advised to beware of the
well-known swindler and confidence trickster
LUIGI BRILLIANTINI
otherwise known as
RED HOT SAM, THE DICE FIEND
and
PRINCE BEDONAILSI, THE INDIAN MYSTIC.
This cunning villain
has escaped from prison in Geneva
and is believed to be in the vicinity.
BE PREPARED!

The sergeant, a great red-faced man with ginger whiskers, nailed this to the wall, stepped back to see if it was straight—and put his foot right in the middle of a cow-pat. When I laughed, he glared at me as if I'd put it there myself, on purpose, and told me to be on my way and not to loiter with intent on the public highway. He always talked like that: in phrases out of the police handbook. Then when he bent over to pick up a stick to clean his boots with, a cart trundling by splashed mud all over the back of his trousers—and just as he stood up to shake his fist and bellow at the driver for using a vehicle in a manner likely to cause a breach of the peace, the door of the police station flew open and out scampered Constable Winkelburg.

The constable was a thin, unhappy-looking man with a droopy mustache, a droopy nose, and droopy shoulders. He was so agitated now that he couldn't stand still but kept jumping from one foot to the other.

"Sergeant! Sergeant! The prisoner—the prisoner—"

"What? What? Get a grip on yourself, Constable! Don't stand there quivering like a jelly! What about the prisoner?"

"He's gone, Sergeant—he's vanished—"

So I decided to vanish, too, and let them find out for themselves that Peter had escaped. It was bound to come out; I was surprised they hadn't discovered it already.

And later, at the castle, I discovered something myself—something that made my blood run colder than it'd run since I'd listened with Peter to the stories of the Demon Hunter through the cracks in the floorboards....

THREE

It was late in the evening, and Lucy and Charlotte had gone to bed. They were in the habit of reading ghostly romances—*The Mysteries of Udolpho*, or *Zastrozzi*, or *Matilda, or The Hermit of the Forest*—until their candle flame sank into the little glassy lake of wax with a sharp whiff of smoke, and darkness fell into the room like a soft, silent avalanche....Scaring each other stiff, in fact. Tonight it was the turn of *Rudolph, or The Phantom of the Crags*. I tucked them up and left them to their horrors, and then climbed the spiral staircase that led to Count Karlstein's study. I was going to ask a favor. Sorry as I'd be to miss the shooting contest, I wanted to ask him if I could go with them as their lady's maid when they went to the hunting lodge. I knew they'd welcome my company; and surely he couldn't object to a simple thing like that?

But I didn't go into the study. I didn't even knock; because when I got to the narrow landing (with the lancet window looking out over the steep leaded roof and the moon blowing along through a wild and gusty sky), I heard him talking. And the first word I heard was: "Zamiel…"

A chilly shiver passed through my heart. That word brought back in an instant all the terrified trembling of my childhood; and it was made worse, not better, for being spoken not in joky terror by Peter, acting the fool, but in the matter-of-fact tones of someone discussing a legal contract. I pinched the candle out and bent to listen closer. Yes, I know I shouldn't have, but I did. And a good thing too.

"Zamiel?" said another voice—a cringing voice, an oily voice, that I knew at once: it belonged to Herr Arturo Snivelwurst, secretary to Count Karlstein and tutor to the girls. A lip-licking, moist-handed, creeping, smarming little ferret, with pomaded hair that he spent half an hour every morning carefully sticking into place so as to look like Napoleon. "Did I hear your grace aright?"

"Zamiel, I said, Snivelwurst," said Count Karlstein. "The Demon Huntsman. The Prince of the Mountains!"

"Ah," said Snivelwurst. "Um."

"Now, listen carefully. For reasons I won't go into now, I have an agreement with that gentleman. Every year on All Souls' Eve he comes to hunt in my forests. He takes whatever prey he likes, and he's welcome to it.…But this year, our agreement runs out and I have to provide—are you listening, Snivelwurst? Are you following me?"

"Like a bloodhound, sir, most eager for the chase!"

"This year," said Count Karlstein, "I have to provide a human prey—"

A gasp (oily) from Snivelwurst; a gasp (stifled) from me, and I clung to the little tin candlestick with both hands as I strained to hear what Count Karlstein said next.

"A living human," he went on, "or two, complete with soul. Now"—he said briskly, and I heard a chair being pulled across the wooden floor and the creak of the ancient floorboards as the count settled down in it—"the question is, who shall it be?"

"Ah, yes, a very vexing question, I can well imagine, your grace. Who shall it be? Indeed! A sorrowful task, picking the right merchandise," said Snivelwurst carefully. He wasn't sure what Karlstein was up to, and he didn't want to say the wrong thing.

"To be sure, Snivelwurst. But in this case there's only one thing for it. It'll have to be my nieces."

A silence then, in which I imagined Snivelwurst putting his finger to his jaw and pretending to consider this suggestion; and in which I nearly sank to the narrow floor in a deadly faint. I'd been cold enough already, Heaven knows, but now I felt as if some cunning mechanism inside me had overturned a bucket of ice-water and let it cascade down the length of my spine. I listened carefully—they were speaking again.

"…quite easy," the count was saying. "The beauty of it

is, there'll be no one about poaching. These damned peasants are so superstitious that none of 'em'll show their warty
noses outside on All Souls' Eve; but even if they did, there
won't be anyone in the forest—they'll all be down in the
village, getting drunk and preparing for the shooting contest!"

"Magnificent!" said the secretary, and I heard a slippery,
shush-shushing noise that puzzled me for a moment until I
realized that he was rubbing his wet hands together. "Truly
Napoleonic, Count Karlstein!"

"Zamiel's going to appear at the hunting lodge at midnight. We'll take 'em there tomorrow, Snivelwurst, stay the
night, come back on Friday—and leave 'em there asleep
with the door locked. That won't keep him out, but it'll
keep them in—eh? His Dark Majesty can gobble 'em up
where they lie, or make 'em scamper through the forest for
a while, as he pleases. *I* shan't miss 'em."

"Oh, nor I, your grace! Pair of hoydens!"

You greasy little liar, I thought. They've never given
you a moment's trouble; lively they might be, especially
Lucy, but for Heaven's sake where's the harm in that? And
to lay them down, sleeping, as an unholy gift for the Demon
Huntsman—that was a plan so evil that the author of
Rudolph, or The Phantom of the Crags herself couldn't have
thought it up. I stood silently, my mind reeling and my
heart beating like a drum. What on earth was I to do now?

Footsteps! The door handle turned! I shrank back against the stone wall and held my breath.

The door opened, the warm light streamed out, and the shuffling, ferrety figure of the secretary hovered in the doorway.

"Never fear, Count Karlstein!" he said, looking back and bobbing his head up and down on his narrow little shoulders. "I shall obey your every command!"

"Of course you will," said Count Karlstein, without any expression at all.

"Good night, sir! Good night!" said Snivelwurst, and pushed the door carefully shut before turning and going down the stairs in a light, tripping scuttle, like a rat in the ballet. Thank Heaven! He didn't see me. I stood quite still for a long time before I dared move, but I had to eventually, as I was shivering so much I was sure I'd drop the candlestick—and that would be the end: I'd find myself in the hunting lodge too, trussed and gagged, wide-eyed in the darkness, waiting for the first ghostly wail of the hunting horns in the midnight sky....

There was nothing for it. I'd have to tell the girls; they'd have to run away. But where, in the name of Heaven, could they go?

I felt my way down the stairs, pausing only to light my candle at the dim fire in the hall before climbing again to the east wing, and to the two rapt faces over their leather-bound book of phantoms.

They were still wide awake. They had a fingernail's-length of candle left and the wick was beginning to lean over, like a sleepy soldier on parade. Lucy pinched it out straight away when I came in with mine, so as to save it for later.

"Hildi, what is it?" said Charlotte. "We heard you coming—we'd just got to the bit where the Phantom appears on the battlements, and we thought—"

I shushed her and she stopped, rather startled, a real person, alive and anxious, being more worrying than a host of phantoms in a book.

"What is it, Hildi?" said Lucy. "You look upset. Have you been to see Susi Dettweiler? Is she hurt badly?"

"No, Miss Lucy, I haven't. But you'll have to listen, now, without interrupting, because this is serious. You understand?"

Lucy sat up, but Charlotte just pulled the quilt around her and watched me with wide eyes. I told them what I'd heard. And they seemed to shrink as I told it: not to get smaller so much as to get younger—more innocent, somehow.

"You'll have to hide, Miss Lucy," I said when I'd finished. "Only till All Souls' Eve; then you can come out again, because the danger'll be past."

"But where can we go?" she said, and I thought: oh, no, she's going to cry. Her voice was shaking and her lip was quivering, and she swallowed hard. But she didn't give way.

"I think I know of a place," I said. "It's a fair way off, but you'll be safe there for a while."

Then Charlotte sat up.

"It's just like *Emilia, or The Poisoned Chalice,*" she said. "She had to run away too, you remember? And then the robber chieftain captures her and they tie her to a stake and—"

"Miss Charlotte, we'll have to get a move on," I said. "Get all your warm clothes and put on everything you can. Cover yourself up tight—it's so cold outside that you'll freeze otherwise."

Lucy jumped out of bed and ran shivering to the great oaken wardrobe. She paused for a second, and then pulled back the heavy curtains across the window. The bedroom overlooked the sheer drop into the valley and the mountains opposite, and the wildness of the scene—though I'd known it all my life—seemed suddenly more harsh, more wild and terrifying, than I could bear. Lucy looked back at me, and in her eyes I could see that she felt the same as I did. It was a fantasy to Charlotte—play, almost. But not to Lucy.

She swallowed hard, again, and began to dress. Charlotte jumped out of bed and did the same, shivering and hopping with chill on the drafty wooden floor. They bundled themselves so thickly with furs and rugs and scarves and hoods that I began to wonder if they'd manage to get through the door; and I filled a bag with spare linen for them.

"Where are we going, Hildi?" said Lucy.

"Are we going to the village?" said Charlotte. "Can we go to your mother's inn? Would she hide us there?"

They liked Ma. She'd looked after them for a day or so when they'd first arrived a year ago, before Count Karlstein found Frau Muller to take charge in the castle, and they'd been so happy to have someone warm and kind nearby, after days of traveling in a strange land among somber grown-up strangers who didn't speak their language, that they'd wept like fountains when she'd had to go back to the Jolly Huntsman. But the inn was full; and besides, it was bound to be the first place to be searched. And then, of course, Peter would be found. I told them what he was doing.

"He's a fugitive from justice!" said Lucy. "He's an outlaw. We won't betray him, don't worry. We know what it's like to be on the run from a cruel fate...."

I hushed her, and helped wide-eyed Charlotte to do up her topmost coat.

"Now, we must be absolutely silent, d'you hear? The count's still awake and Herr Snivelwurst is bound to be creeping about somewhere. We'll leave the castle through the stables and slide down that rocky slope beyond the wall until it meets the road lower down. But not a word!"

It wasn't until we were outside in the biting cold, with the wind searching out all the gaps in my threadbare old cloak and lashing my hair across my eyes, that I thought: what am I going to do? Am I going to run away with them, or am I going to go back and pretend that I know nothing about it?

After some time we rounded a corner in the road and came to a fork. One branch led down to the village and over the bridge to the square—half an hour's easy walk, with lighted windows at the end of it, singing from the tavern, and the church snoozing dimly under a snowy quilt. The other branch of the road led along the side of the valley, to a pass where, at this time of year, the snow was too deep for travelers. I hesitated for a second or two as we stood at the fork, for the village looked so welcoming; and then the moon came out from behind a shark-shaped cloud and lit up the rocky wildness of the landscape. And I turned away from the village, for the moonlight showed me a glimpse of the place we were heading for.

High up on the slope to our right, in among the trees, a little frozen waterfall glinted brilliantly. A short way beyond it, as I knew very well, was a cave—the hermit's cave, we used to call it, because many years ago there'd lived a poor old man in there, a gentle mad soul who used to talk to himself all day long, believing himself to be a dancing bear who for the love of the Virgin Mary had given up entertaining folks and taken to praying for them instead; but who still needed commanding, like a bear, so he'd say, "Good boy, Bruno, on your knees now, pray, that's a good bear—fold your paws—shut your eyes—there's a good bear—up you get, then...." We used to take him honey-cakes once in a while, which he'd feed to himself as a reward for praying well, and then in his old bear's shuffle he'd lumber forward and slump to his knees beside us and lick our hands gently, telling himself to pray for us....The sweetest souls in the world are those that aren't fully in it. I thought: old Bruno'll look after us. I meant his spirit, of course, since he'd died when I was seven.

"This way," I said, and we took the upper road.

Where it crossed the stream we left the road itself and followed the bouncing waterway through the tangled brambles, the rocks and bushes and hollows full of wet snow, climbing all the time, until we were nearly at the waterfall. Then we took off our shoes (soaked through now, anyway) and stockings, and stepped gingerly into the dark water. It wasn't deeper anywhere than our knees, and even Charlotte could have lain with her head on one bank and her feet on the other; but the stones at the bottom were sharp and painful and the water was worse than cold: it was deadly. We stumbled across, holding our shoes and stockings in numb, shaking hands, until our feet could bear it no longer, and we hopped out, crying with the pain of it. We slapped each other's feet and ankles until the blood unfroze and we could move them again, then put our wet shoes and stockings back on.

"That should throw the hounds off the scent, anyway," said Lucy in satisfaction—at least, that's what she meant to say, but her teeth were chattering so much she might have been speaking in Turkish.

We came to the waterfall, and gasped, not with cold— for we were beyond gasping with that—but with astonishment. A thick crust of spiky, sugary, bristly spears glinted and shone in the moonlight, all set about with a million tiny diamond-sharp stars of frost; and under it somewhere, the little stream tinkled in a subdued sort of way, like a child put grumbling to bed too early for its liking. The world by moonlight could be lovely as well as threatening; the sky was clear, now, of those lean and wolfish clouds and seemed almost serene.

"Only a little way further," I said, to cheer them on.

The path to Bruno's cave was a little overgrown and I couldn't find it at first. But soon I had it, and five minutes later we were nearly in the clearing, talking cheerfully about getting warm again. When—

"Shhh!" Lucy held her hand up.

We stopped.

"What is it?" whispered Charlotte.

I turned my head so as to hear it more clearly, for I'd heard something, too. From the cave.

The unmistakable sound of a snore…a full, deep one. A man's snore. We'd arrived too late: the cave was already tenanted. Lucy looked at me, her eyes full of fear.

"What shall we do?" she whispered.

But I didn't have to answer, because as she spoke the snorer gave a sudden grunt and the snoring stopped.

And a voice from the cave said: "Who's there?"

FOUR

We were too frightened even to shiver. Charlotte's hand was clutching mine as if it had frozen there and was stuck for good; and through my mind went galloping a dozen or more brigands, robbers, outlaws, and cut-throats, all with blazing eyes and armed with knives and guns. We stood like stone.

After a moment there came the sound of something stirring in the cave—dry leaves, perhaps, rustling; and another voice spoke.

"What is it, you booby?" came calmly out of the darkness, in a clear, rich voice of the sort that actors have: an expressive voice, with a hint of the mountebank about it. "The fleas disturbing you? To deal with fleas, my dear Max, you have only to crack them between your fingernails. They expire in silence. You do not have to make speeches to them and challenge them like a sentry."

"No, I heard a voice, Doctor," said the first man. "There's someone outside, creeping about."

"Fiddlesticks. I have been lying awake here for hours, meditating on my destiny, and I heard nothing at all but your melodious and trombone-like snorings. You were dreaming of the applause, the roars of acclaim, the demands for an encore, that will follow our performance tomorrow. Go back to sleep, Max; resume your snores."

"Well, you may be right, Doctor; but I *did* hear something...."

Silence; then presently, indeed, the snores began again. We relaxed, and tiptoed out of the clearing and back down the path to the waterfall. There we sat on a convenient (if icy) rock and whispered.

"What do we do now?" said Lucy.

"Who were they?" said Charlotte.

"How does Hildi know who they were, stupid?" said Lucy. "They're robbers, obviously."

"That other man said something about a performance," said Charlotte. "They might be actors! They wouldn't hurt us—they might even let us stay in their cave!"

I thought so, too—but you could never tell. Actors or performing players or traveling showmen are slippery folk, all charm and greasepaint. We'd played host to them often enough at the Jolly Huntsman, and sometimes been paid in coins whose gold wore off as soon as the players' coach had trundled out of reach; or found that our good linen sheets had changed, by some artistic process, into torn, drab cotton in the course of a single night. No: these two in the cave sounded harmless enough—but I didn't trust them, all the same.

"It'll have to be the mountain guide's hut, Miss Lucy," I said. "Another hour's walk…but it's that much safer, being further up, like…."

"Another *hour?*" said Charlotte; and indeed she was nearly dropping with fatigue. All the excitement had drained away, and I think she'd have taken the chance of facing the Demon Huntsman himself for the sake of a soft, warm bed just then.

"You've got to," I said, a little roughly. "Miss Lucy, too. And don't forget—I'll have to be back at the castle tomorrow and pretend I don't know anything about you being missing. You can just lie low in the hut and snooze all day long if you want to. Come on, it's getting late."

I pulled Charlotte to her feet, and the three of us began to trudge up the slope again, through the bushes and the tangled undergrowth beside the stream, until we came out onto the bare hillside higher up. We didn't speak; not so much because we needed to be silent up here as because we didn't have enough breath left to make words out of.

We found the mountain guide's hut, unlocked as it always was and with a pile of dry firewood (no use to us, though, without a tinderbox), the straw mattresses and the wooden beds all ready for any poor traveler who found himself snowbound up here. Lucy exclaimed with delight at the neatness of it, but Charlotte could say nothing, being worn out; so I laid her on one of the beds, took off her shoes and stockings (which were still wet from the icy stream), rubbed her legs dry, and put dry stockings on her before covering her with another of the mattresses, so that she looked like a little mountain of softly rustling straw. But she didn't know what she looked like: she was asleep. Within a minute, so was Lucy; and sometime later, so was I— wondering ruefully as my eyes closed how many precious minutes would fly past before the dawn came and woke me.

It felt like no more than five. It was dark still, but the air had the stirring, impatient feel it gets just before daybreak, and there was some self-important bird chirruping bossily outside. I lay still for a moment. Then the running stream and the sound of the girls' breathing woke me— jerked me fully awake, as a handclap might have done. I sat up: what was the time? Would I manage to get back to the castle before everyone woke up?

I got up and put on my shoes, gathering my thin old cloak tightly around myself to keep out as much of the chill air as possible, and shook Lucy's shoulder gently.

"Miss Lucy! Miss Lucy! I've got to go now! I've got to get back to the castle. But I'll be back later—if I can!"

"Oh, you *must*, Hildi...." She was awake now, but not so much as I was; yawning and rubbing her eyes, her face pale with anxiety. "You must come back—we wouldn't know what to do otherwise—"

"I'll try!" I whispered, not to awaken Charlotte, who stirred and pulled the straw mountain further over herself. "I'll really try my very hardest, I promise! But with Frau Muller bossing me about, it's going to be hard to get away—I tell you what, though," I said, as an idea came to me: "If *I* can't come, I'll get someone else to come up here with some food and a tinderbox—how's that?"

"How will we know who they are? It might be a trick," she said, struggling to sit up. "We'll need a password!"

"Yes, all right—but I'll have to go in a second—"

"Let me think—oh, what shall it be?" She fluttered her hands, and put them to her mouth, as her sleepy eyes opened wide with the effort of thinking; and then she said, "Cheltenham!"

It wasn't a word I knew, and I tried to say it so as not to forget it. "What's it mean?" I said.

She told me it was the name of a place in England, where she and Charlotte had attended a ladies' school. I promised her I wouldn't forget; and said that someone—either me or someone else (though I couldn't imagine who, unless I persuaded my brother, Peter, to leave the cellar)—would come up to the hut later on, with food and drink and

38

something to light a fire with. She nodded, and curled up again under the straw, asleep in a moment.

The sky was lightening rapidly. I'd have to hurry if I wanted to be back at the castle before anyone found out I'd been missing. I ran down the side of the mountain, shoved my way through the forest, and scampered up the road as fast as if Zamiel himself was after me, and arrived (entering through the stables, the way we'd left, with the warm horses shifting restlessly as a wet, shivery, breathless figure tiptoed through the midst of them and peered cautiously into the courtyard) just as the bell in the tower tolled six. It couldn't be better; that was the time I normally awoke.

Five minutes or so to get up to my bedroom under the drafty tiles of the roof, change my clothes, and dash downstairs into the kitchen to begin my chores. Sticks for the fire, water from the well, pump away with the bellows till the fire blazed good and hot, take a shovelful of red embers into Frau Muller's parlor and light her fire with them, do the same for the fire in the great hall, put a pan of water on the kitchen fire to boil for Frau Muller's coffee (which she had before all the rest of the household), prepare a tray for the count's coffee, set out the cutlery for the servants' breakfast (not much needed; it was porridge all round, and thin stuff too, since Frau Muller had her breakfast with us and kept a miser's eye on the cream and sugar), and finally lay the table for the family's breakfast.

By this time, the other servants were up and about. Frau Wenzel was stirring the porridge in the kitchen; Frau Muller was sipping her coffee and studying the day's menus and the list of jobs to be done around the place. And now I had to learn to be an actress; for the next thing I had to do, on a normal morning, was to go and wake the girls.

I shook the empty beds, and drew back the curtains. "Miss Lucy! Miss Charlotte!" I called, but not too loudly, yet.

No reply, of course. I waited a moment, then called again, louder; looked under the beds, in the wardrobe, in the bathroom, in the corridor, in the empty rooms that stood dustily nearby; called again, and let (with great artistry) a note of fright into my voice.

"Miss Lucy! Miss Charlotte! Where are you?"

Now for the audience, I thought; and ran downstairs.

"Frau Muller! Miss Lucy and Miss Charlotte—they're not there!"

"Where? What do you mean, girl?"

"They're not upstairs, in their beds—I can't find them anywhere—"

And so on. Within ten minutes, every servant in the castle had been pressed into the search, and Herr Snivelwurst scuttled up to tell the count. I didn't relish the idea of what he'd have to say. Together with all the other servants, I bustled through the rooms upstairs, the attics, the cellars, the stables—calling their names down every corridor and up every staircase, and acting furiously all the time. The longer we spent on this, of course, the safer they'd be; it was when the search spread out beyond the grounds that they'd be in danger. But I might still distract it a little.

"Your grace," I said to the count, as he gnawed the fingers of his right hand, while his left held a great beaker of coffee laced with brandy; he was standing in the hall, shouting orders at every servant who came in sight, his face growing more thunderous by the minute. "Your grace, I think I know where they might have gone."

"What? Where? Speak up, hussy!"

I curtsied nervously and said, "Through the village, sir, and into the Schelkhorn Valley, if you please."

"What for? How do you know? Are you involved in this?"

"Oh, no, sir! But they were talking about the river, sir, and how they'd like to follow it to the lake, if you please. They might have gone out for a game and lost their way down there. There were some gypsies going that way yesterday...."

Gypsies! They got the blame for everything, from the disappearance of the little heir twenty years before, to this. There weren't any gypsies there at all, of course, but it might throw him off the scent for a little while.

The count glared at me, and I thought for a moment that he was going to strike me; his fists were clenched, and the mug of coffee shook and spilled some of its bitter contents with a hiss into the ashes of the fire he stood by; but he turned abruptly and called: "Lentz! Schaffner!"

These were Johann the footman and Adolphus the groom. They came running, and he ordered them to set off with guns down through the village toward the Schelkhorn Valley. "This girl will come with you," he said. "If she's too slow for you, leave her behind. I want those girls back today, you understand?" And he turned swiftly and went off to call up all the other servants: the huntsmen, the one old gardener, the kennel-master, the coachman—everyone he could find, while I flung on my old threadbare cloak, still wet from the night's exertions, and ran off down the road after Johann and Adolphus.

It was a fine sunny morning, and they were full of the glee of the hunt. They were quite willing to accept my suggestions as to where they should search and equally willing to let me stay behind in the village. So I left them at the bridge; they went off whistling, and I ran on into the parlor of the Jolly Huntsman. But before I even entered the building, I heard a rare old commotion. I paused inside the door and rubbed my eyes in surprise.

A line of strangers, arguing, jostling, gesturing, with

three or four different languages on the go at once, was queuing up in front of Sergeant Snitsch, who sat at our biggest table, looking very stern, more flustered than stern, and more pompous than flustered.

"Next!" he shouted, and the man at the head of the queue stepped forward and showed him some papers. I didn't know what it could be about, so I went into the kitchen and asked Ma.

"Search me," she said. "The sergeant's got some silly idea that there's a famous criminal about, so he's got everyone in the tavern to come and show him their papers. What a fuss! And I dread to think what Peter must be doing down there—he'll be listening to all the noise, and he'll be dying to come up and have a look, and I daren't go down and tell him what's going on in case the sergeant takes it into his head to come into the kitchen. Oh, I could throttle that boy, I could honestly! The trouble he's caused! And what are you doing down here, anyway? That lady sent you down here for her bags, has she?"

"What lady?" I said; I was trying to get a word in edgewise and tell her about the girls, in the hope that she might be able to help—but now she was peering through the kitchen door again. "Ma!" I called her. "What lady d'you mean?"

"Hasn't she come up to the castle, then? I thought you'd have met her on the way down. The sergeant sent her off with Constable Winkelburg, because she didn't have the right papers, and she told him what to do with himself—powerful way with words, she had—and she said to one and all that she was going to escape from the constable and that no one was going to prevent her from going up to the castle to pay her respects to Count Karlstein and visit her girls."

"Her girls? For goodness' sake, who is she?"

"Miss Davenport, her name is. She used to be a teacher in England—Cheltenheim, or somewhere. She used to teach Miss Lucy and Miss Charlotte. She's traveling, and she thought she'd call in and pay 'em a visit—why, what's the matter?"

Because I'd had to sit down in astonishment. Their teacher! Come to see them! And now she was going up to the castle, and—

I'd have to go and talk to her. If I hurried, I might be able to catch her. "Which way did Constable Winkelburg take her?" I said.

"I don't know! The sergeant just said to take her to the parish boundary and leave her there. He was getting a bit cross, and as soon as this lady spoke up to him, he thought he'd better take a firm line. You know how he is. Such a shame—she was a nice lady, too, and she'd only just arrived. But she said she'd been in tighter places than this: that she'd been exploring in Borneo and the king of the headhunters had condemned her to death, and that she'd shot him and escaped! You should have seen the constable's face!"

"Ma, listen...." And I told her the whole thing.

She sat down and her mouth opened wide with amazement. Finally she held up her hand. "I won't hear another word," she said. "And I'm not having you going down the cellar and stirring up that brother of yours, either. He'd like nothing better than an excuse to go tearing over the mountains on a wild-goose chase. He's in trouble with the law, don't you understand? And that's *real* trouble, not some nonsense about ghosts and spirits and demon huntsmen. You get off up the mountain and bring those poor little girls back to the castle. You've frightened them out of their wits with these tales of yours—now go and get them back! Go on!"

She didn't believe me....And now she was angry. Oh, it wasn't all anger; I knew that well enough. There was worry in it, too, both for Peter and for the two girls—and for me, because she could see me getting into trouble and losing my position at the castle. There was nothing to be done.

"All right, I'll go," I said, knowing I'd do nothing of the sort. I stood up. "But you won't tell anyone, will you?"

"You're a silly girl," was all the reply I got to that; so I turned to go.

I went through the kitchen door into the parlor—and heard a voice that stopped me dead.

The kitchen door was right next to the foot of the stairs, and someone—two men were coming down the staircase as I came through the door. I looked up. I'd never seen them before; they were obviously new guests, come for the shooting contest. They looked into the parlor, saw what Sergeant Snitsch was doing, and paused. Neither of them saw me, because the door into the kitchen was set back a little way, in the shadows; and one of the men said to the other: "Look, Max—that fat fool's inspecting papers...."

It was the man from the cave!

FIVE

I didn't move.

"Have you got any papers, Doctor Cadaverezzi?" said the other man quietly, the one called Max.

"Not yet," said the first man. He was the one with the actor's voice, and he looked like an actor, too; he was wearing a large broadbrimmed hat with a great sweeping feather in it, and a long black cloak. Max, the servant (or so I guessed), was dressed more simply. He had an honest, cheerful face, and I thought: If only we'd known that last night—I'm sure he wouldn't have hurt us....The doctor's face was handsome, I couldn't deny that: dark, powerful features, strong white teeth, and glittering eyes—but again that quality of actorishness came into my mind. He's impressive, I thought, but I don't trust him.

"What are we going to do, then?" said Max.

"Leave it to me," said the doctor. "Nothing could be easier." And he sauntered casually to the end of the queue and tapped some stranger on the shoulder. The stranger looked round, and the doctor pointed through the window and said something to make him stare in that direction; and while he was doing that, the doctor slipped his hand into the stranger's pocket and drew out his papers. You villain! I thought. He'll get into trouble now, all because of you....But I couldn't help watching, to see what would happen next. Max sat down at the foot of the stairs, only an arm's length away from where I stood in the shadows.

The doctor reached the front of the queue; the stranger was still searching his pockets, mystified. When the sergeant had inspected the papers, the doctor beckoned him to follow. They came toward the stairs; I pretended to be dusting in the corner.

"I imagine," said the doctor smoothly as the sergeant came up, "that you are looking for Brilliantini?"

(Brilliantini? Where had I heard that name before? Oh, yes! The confidence trickster who'd escaped from prison. Surely this couldn't be him?)

The sergeant stared to left and right and then thrust his head forward, whiskers bristling, and said in a low voice, "Yes! But how do you know?"

"I am a member of the Venetian Secret Service," said the doctor. "Very confidential, you understand."

"Oh! My word! Yes!"

"I, too, am looking for this villain. He is wanted for several desperate crimes in Venice."

"Good heavens!"

"He is very dangerous, you understand?"

"Is he, really?"

"He would shoot you as soon as look at you, Sergeant. I advise you not to get close to him."

"Well, I never…"

"We had better work together on this case. I shall give all my information to you, and you can tell me everything that you know."

"Good idea!"

"There is a reward for his capture—I suppose you were told by the authorities?"

"A reward, eh? Er—how much might that be, then, if you don't mind my asking?"

"For anyone who aids in his capture, the State has ordered that a medal be especially struck."

The sergeant's eyes lit up and his chest thrust itself forward, as if the medal was already twinkling on the front of it. "A medal, eh?" he said.

"Yes," said the doctor solemnly. "The Order of the Golden Banana."

"Oh! My word!"

"So—be discreet, eh, Sergeant? Not a word to a soul?"

"Wouldn't dream of it, sir!"

"And tell me everything you find out—every single thing."

"Certainly, sir! Me and my constable are at your service, sir! Don't you worry, we'll have him under lock and key before he can turn around!"

The sergeant saluted smartly, turned around himself—and fell over the rug, crashing full length to the floor. His helmet, with the long spike on the top, rolled under the table where Rudi Gallmeyer, one of Peter's friends, was sitting. Rudi picked up the helmet, polishing it furiously on his sleeve, and set it on the sergeant's head.

"Thank you, Gallmeyer," said the sergeant sternly. "Glad to see someone's got some manners in this place." And he stalked out proudly, quite unaware that the fresh gale of laughter that followed him was caused by the apple that Rudi had stuck on the spike before returning his helmet.

Doctor Cadaverezzi watched all this with amusement, and then turned to Max. "I don't think we'll have any trouble with him," he said.

And then he saw me. And winked! He must have known I'd overheard him. I didn't know what to say. I knew he was Brilliantini and he knew I knew, and yet he didn't seem in the least worried about it. He had a sublime, innocent confidence that overlay all his deceptive ways and turned them into play. He crooked his finger, beckoning me.

"What's your name, young lady?" he said.

"Hildi, sir."

"You work here, do you?"

"No, sir—I work up at the castle, but I come down here to help my mother sometimes...."

"Ah, good. Then would you give her my compliments and ask her if she will display this poster where it will be seen by all the customers?" Like a conjurer, he whisked a large roll out of his sleeve and handed it to me with a bow, sweeping his hat low along the ground with his other hand. I unrolled it.

AN EXHIBITION

of

DOCTOR CADAVEREZZI'S

CABINET OF WONDERS!

will shortly be given

ON THESE PREMISES.

MARVELS!

WONDERS OF THE NATURAL WORLD!

Scientifical, Magical, Philosophical,
Mechanical, Spiritual, and Artistical Phenomena
of a QUALITY and SPLENDOR

NEVER BEFORE SEEN!!

EXHIBITED *to Tumultuous Applause*
Before the CROWNED HEADS
of

FOUR CONTINENTS!

"Are you putting on a show, sir?" I said.

"This very evening!"

I was entranced. There was nothing I'd have liked better than to see his Cabinet of Wonders; but how could I, with Lucy and Charlotte to look after, up in their mountain hut with no food—and Count Karlstein raging up and down like a madman, looking for them? Doctor Cadaverezzi and Max were speaking together, quietly, and I took the poster in to Ma. She was as pleased as I was; she loved a show, which was why she never turned actors away in spite of their artistic habits. I made her promise to tell me all about it, and then hurried out.

But no sooner had I stepped through into the parlor than I hastily took a step backward again into the shadow; for there, talking earnestly to Max, was that cringing rascal Herr Snivelwurst.

"Excuse me, my man," he said, smirking, "but have you by any chance seen two little girls in the recent past?"

"Two little girls?" said Max, looking puzzled. "How little?"

"Ten years and twelve years, respectively. Their names are Charlotte and Lucy, and they've been very naughty and run away from their loving home, and I've been ordered by their kind uncle to offer a reward for bringing 'em back again...."

I caught my breath when I heard this and I think I put

my hand to my mouth; at any rate, Max saw me and looked past Snivelwurst's shoulder. And seeing where he was looking, the secretary turned round as well.

"Ah!" he said, flapping his skinny fingers, trying to remember my name. "Er—um! Looking for the girls, are you?"

"Yes, Herr Snivelwurst," I said.

"Where do I bring 'em, supposing I finds 'em?" said Max.

"Up to the castle, young man. Ask for Count Karlstein. But you're not to take any notice of what those girls'll tell you. Very artful they are, very imaginative, full of stories. Don't listen to a word of it! Grab hold of the little perishers and bring 'em on up to the castle, and Count Karlstein'll see to it that you don't go away any the poorer. You won't lose by it, I promise you that!"

"Oh, right, I'll do that!" said Max, and I shook my head at him desperately. "I could do with some money right now. Are you all right, miss?"

"Yes—yes," I said miserably. I'd have to find some way of speaking to him on his own. He looked friendly enough; I was sure he'd believe me, even if no one else did. But I didn't have the chance, because Snivelwurst tucked my hand beneath his arm; Max went briskly out of the tavern one way, and we went the other.

"Come with me, my dear!" said the secretary. "You

may walk up to the castle with me—you'll enjoy that."

I dragged my feet, I pretended to have a stone in my shoe, I pretended I'd forgotten something and would have to run back for it—I even thought of fainting, but I look too healthy to get away with that. He clung to me like ivy.

"It must be very pleasant for you, to have some cultured conversation," he said. "I'm a person of considerable education, you know."

"Really? Oh, dear—listen to the church bell! Is that the time? I'll have to run on and get Count Karlstein's lunch—"

"Don't you worry about that, my dear; he's out with the hounds, so he won't be lunching at the castle. Now, let me point out some of the interesting sights of the valley for you…you might not have noticed them before. Not all eyes are as sharp as mine! Ha, ha!"

Oh! It was unbearable. How in the world could I escape from him? On and on he went, telling me about things I'd known all my life—and getting most of them wrong—and all in a tone of such greasy helpfulness that it would have choked a shark to try and swallow it.

But finally I saw a way of getting rid of him. It was drastic, but it worked. The river ran along beside the road for a little way, and I pointed into the water and said, "Ooh, look! Look at that fish, Herr Snivelwurst! What sort is it?"

"I'm by way of being an expert on natural history, my

dear—you've asked the right man, ha, ha! Let me just step down onto this prominent rock—"

And as soon as his back was turned, I pushed him in. He roared and squealed and splashed, and I shrieked as if in dismay.

"Oh! Herr Snivelwurst, you've fallen in!"

"I know! I know I've fallen in! Help me out! Help! Help!"

"Oh, you're drowning, Herr Snivelwurst—you're going under—oh, I can't bear to watch!"

"Oh—oh—oh! It's freezing cold! Help, don't stand there shrieking! Pull me out!"

"But—but I don't know what to do! I'll have to run and get help! Don't go away! I'll bring some men with ropes and things!"

"No—no! Don't! Help me out—oh, oh, oh, it's cold!" But I'd turned to go and was running as fast as I could back toward the village as his bubbling cries rose out of the river behind me. I hoped he *didn't* drown—not that there was much danger of that, because the river was shallow and he'd been sitting on the rocky bottom as he yelled and squeaked for help. He might catch a cold, but it'd serve him right.

I was soon out of breath. I seemed to have done nothing since yesterday but run and climb and feel frightened. Everything was going wrong. Why was it so difficult to keep

two little girls hidden for a day or so? But I had to keep trying—there was no choice in the matter. If only I could find
Max before he found the girls, I might be able to enlist his
help….

I did. I found him around the very next corner in the
road. But someone else had found him too: a young woman,
dressed as a lady's maid, with a smart coat of brown worsted
and a neat little fur-trimmed hood….And they were making the most of this chance meeting, if that's what it was,
because their arms were around each other and they were
kissing as if it had just been invented and they'd been asked
to try it out. I stopped still, in despair; what could I do now?
I couldn't interrupt, could I? I wouldn't be welcomed, that
was plain; but what else could I do?

I sat down beside a tree, on a dry stone that stuck up out
of the snow, and waited for them to notice me.

"Oh, Maxie," said the girl, at last.

"Oh, Eliza! Fancy running into you like this! Where's
your mistress?"

"They arrested her, Maxie! I didn't know what to do!
They were inspecting papers or something, and she didn't
have the right sort, and the fat sergeant sent a little skinny
constable out to escort her to the parish boundary—but
she went tearing off so fast, dragging him along behind her,
that I couldn't follow them!"

So her mistress must be…the girls' old teacher! So

she'd be bound to listen! Or—would she? As a teacher, wouldn't she think that anything to do with the Demon Huntsman was that dreaded thing, Imagination? Wouldn't she think that the best place for the girls was back in the castle, under the care of Count Karlstein? And so—hadn't I better *not* tell this Eliza about it all? Oh, I didn't know *what* to do!

"You've still got your trombone, Maxie?" she said fondly.

"It ain't a trombone, Eliza, it's a coach-horn," he said proudly.

"And your lovely coach, Max! Have you still got it? Is that how you came here?"

"No, me love; I had an accident in Geneva. It was all because of a plate of sausages...." They strolled off slowly, arm in arm. I followed them; I couldn't help it.

"A plate of sausages?" said Eliza.

"That's right," said Max mournfully. "After I set you and Miss Davenport down in Geneva, I went into a tavern to have a plate of sausages and some beer, to take me mind off the sorrow of parting from you, like. Well, I had me musket with me and I set it down on the floor beside the table, to be safe, see? But when the serving girl came with the sausages, I caught me foot in the trigger, and it was loaded, only I'd forgotten—and it went off and shot the leg off an old gentleman's chair."

"No!"

"And as he fell backward, he grabbed at the table, see, and upset me plate—and a steaming hot sausage flew into the air and landed down the serving girl's neck! And so she dropped the candle what she was carrying—and it set light to me britches...."

"Oh, Maxie!"

"So there was only one thing to do—I ran outside, yelling at one end and blazing at the other, and I jumped into the trough where old Jenny was drinking. She didn't recognize her master, I suppose, in the heat of the moment, like, and she set off down the marketplace, upsetting stalls, with eggs and apples everywhere—and ran straight into the lake, poor girl, with the coach and all."

"Oh, poor old Jenny! Was she all right?"

"Yes, they got her out, but that was the end of the coach. And there was me, sitting in the horse trough, with the serving girl and the old gentleman and the landlord all setting on me at once—and I stood up to defend meself, and then—that was when they arrested me."

"Arrested you! Whatever for?"

"Well, when I stood up, I found me britches had all burned away. Very strict about britches they are, in Geneva. I had to sell poor old Jenny and the musket as well, to pay for the damage to the market, and I got thirty days in jail for appearing in public with no britches."

"Oh, poor old Max!"

"I fell on me feet in jail, though, Eliza. I met a gent in there what had been jailed by mistake—that's what he said, anyway. Doctor Cadaverezzi's his name. He's a traveling showman, and he's got a Cabinet of Wonders. He took me on as his personal servant and magical assistant! But what that all means, my little dove, is that I ain't got any money at the moment—and I can't marry you as soon as we planned...."

"Oh, Maxie!"

And then they seemed to have forgotten what kissing was like, so they tried it again, just to remind themselves. I thought: I shouldn't be listening to this. They're a nice couple—they don't deserve to be overheard....

"I've still got that present you gave me, Maxie!" she said, after a moment or two. "That funny little broken coin on a chain." She fished it out from inside the neck of her dress and showed him.

"I couldn't afford a ring, Eliza," he said, "but that's precious, that coin, I've had that since I was a tiny baby. It's a token of my love, me love."

More kissing....

They won't look for the girls, I thought; they'll spend all day mooning up and down with their arms round each other. I don't think they'd have seen me then if I'd jumped out in the road in front of them, pulling faces, waggling my fingers in front of my nose, and blowing raspberries.

No, there was only one person who could help Lucy and Charlotte, and that was me.

SIX

And all I could do was wonder when I'd be able to go up the mountain with some food and a tinderbox, between all the other chores I had to do; for there's no one busier than a maidservant.

No sooner had I reached the castle, for instance, than Frau Muller snapped at me, "Where've you been? How am I supposed to run a staff of servants if they all take the morning off whenever they feel like it? There's a lady come to see the count and no one to wait on them. Get out of that filthy old cloak and take them some wine—hurry up, girl!"

"Who is it?" I said, dropping my cloak over the back of Frau Wenzel's chair and smoothing my hair down. "I thought he was out with the hounds?"

"What's it to do with you? He went out and came back again. Your trouble is, you don't know your place. Too friendly with those two little perishers who ran off—good riddance, says I. You've got ideas above your station, Hildi

Kelmar. Get on up to the drawing-room, and don't keep them waiting any longer."

I hastened up there nervously. Count Karlstein was standing by the fireplace, and a plump, warmly dressed woman of about thirty-five or so sat very upright in the best chair. I wasn't sure who she was yet, but something about her reminded me of the girls—some foreign air—and something else reminded me of Meister Haifisch: some steely toughness in her eyes; and she was distinctly pretty in a brisk kind of way. She looked at me with bright curiosity, as if she was about to speak and thinking better of it. What's more, she looked at ease and the count didn't.

"Can I offer you some refreshment, Miss Davenport?" he said.

Of course! I thought. Miss Davenport!

"How kind," she said. "I am exhilarated by the walk on this fine morning. I shall take a little mineral water, thank you so much."

Her accent was strong, but although some of her phrases sounded odd, she spoke confidently. The count seemed a little taken aback at the idea of anyone wanting to drink water, and he couldn't help making a face as she said it— rude man. I curtsied, but before I could go out, she said, "Perhaps the maid could summon the girls, for me to greet them? I shall not be long in the district, after all."

I looked at Count Karlstein.

"I'm very sorry," he said harshly. "That's out of the question. They're ill, both of them." He looked uneasy as he said it. Strange that such a villain could be such a poor liar! She knew he was lying, too. I could see her sit a little forward on her chair, and her eyes sparkled.

"I'm sorry to hear that, Count Karlstein. What are they suffering from?"

"A fever," said the count.

"Then you must let me look at them. I have no medical degree, of course, but I have studied privately under Professor Wurmhoell of Heidelberg. Tell me, who is supervising their treatment, Count Karlstein? Allow me to see their physician. I shall wait for refreshment until I have examined the girls. The maid can take me to their chamber," she said, sweeping to her feet and bearing down on me.

Good for you! I thought, but then the count leaped forward as if he'd stepped in the fire by mistake.

"No! No! Out of the question! I could not possibly allow it! Their condition is perfectly safe, but they must not be allowed any contact from outside the valley. To expose them to the influence of travelers, even learned ones, Miss Davenport, who have passed through less healthy places on their journeys—no, no, I cannot allow it. A great pity—but there you are. I would be failing in my duty if I let you see them."

Miss Davenport was watching him closely. He looked in need of medical treatment himself: deathly pale, bristling with nerves, his face silvered by a light panicky sweat. Miss Davenport looked at him as if he were a specimen of some new tropical plant. He tried to outface her, and had to turn away; and she demurely sat down again.

"Of course, you're right, Count Karlstein," she said. "Quite the best thing to do." She folded her hands on her lap and looked at me. The count had his back to me, and I was able to shake my head vigorously for a moment. Then he turned and saw me.

"Go and fetch the water, girl," he said, waving his hand to dismiss me.

I hurried away. When I came back they were talking politely about the weather, or something. I heard the count ask where she was going to stay and I pricked up my ears before I was sent out again; but all I heard was something to the effect that since she'd come equipped for a journey of scientific exploration (and had only broken her travels here for a day or so) she was perfectly happy to camp, like a Red Indian, I supposed, the tavern being full and the village barred to her by Sergeant Snitsch. Then the count glared at me, and I curtsied and left.

I must speak to her, I thought. But some evil power (I was becoming convinced) was frustrating all my good intentions. Because when I got back to the kitchen, I was met by Frau Wenzel the cook, beside herself with excitement and weeping with joy.

"Oh, Hildi! Oh, Hildi! Isn't it wonderful?" she sobbed.

"What? For goodness' sake, what is it?"

"They've found Miss Charlotte! They've brought her back, all safe and sound!"

I sat down, astonished. No, it wasn't wonderful at all. I was furious. I knew what had happened—they'd left the hut, stupid things, and she'd been caught.

"Where is she now?" I said. "I'll go and see her. She'll want—"

"Kelmar!" said the voice of Frau Muller, and her goose-shaped figure swept into the kitchen like a cold draft. "That brat's been found. She's in the tower, and she's not to be seen to, d'you hear? You're not to go near her."

"But where's she been? What happened? And why—"

"Just do as you're told!" she snapped. "I think you know more than you pretend. If you go near that child, I'll have you tanned, don't think I won't. And it won't stop there." She cast a suspicious look around the kitchen, and swept out as swiftly as she'd swept in.

"Why mustn't I go up to her?" I said to Frau Wenzel, who was fanning her face weakly with the day's menus.

"Oh, dear, oh, dear, I wouldn't argue with her—she's got a terrible temper, and it's me'll get the rough edge of her tongue. It's not fair, Hildi, what I have to put up with in here—I wouldn't get it anywhere else, not treatment like this...." A sniff or two, another sob, and she was over the worst of that; and while she stirred a pot of stew, I sat at the table and chopped up some carrots and got the story out of her.

It seemed that while Miss Davenport had been upstairs with Count Karlstein, a very watery gentleman had turned up at the castle gate, dripping and shivering and leaking badly—and clinging tightly to a chilly little girl. Herr Snivelwurst, clambering painfully out of the rocky torrent I'd shoved him into, had seen Charlotte emerging from the woods. He'd never have caught her if he'd given chase; but he had the presence of mind (and absence of decency) to lie down and yell....

And she, seeing what looked like a sorely distressed traveler at the side of the road, remembered the story of the Good Samaritan and came up to help; and found a fishy hand tight around her wrist and an oily grin of triumph leering up at her. And so he'd brought her back—but apparently she'd said nothing about where Lucy might be, or about why they'd gone in the first place. And Herr Snivelwurst was now sitting with his bony feet in a bowl of hot water by the fire in Frau Muller's private parlor, with a blanket around his skinny shoulders, bright-eyed with heroism and brandy. Pity I didn't push him under with a stick, I thought, while I had the chance.

Charlotte had been locked in the lumber room beneath the count's study—as a punishment, Frau Wenzel said, for wickedness. And did I have a moment to get up there? I did not. Frau Muller kept me busy all the rest of the morning. My spirits lowered with every minute that passed, and as soon as lunch was over she set me the task of cleaning all the silver—even the great soup tureen, ornamented with lumpy dolphins and fat little mermaids, that had never been used since I'd been at the castle. It all came out of its baize and sat depressingly on the kitchen table, and I sat in front of it and rubbed away with the fine sand until every little speck of tarnish had disappeared. I knew where it had gone, too—my heart was as dull and dark as the silver itself had been, by the time I'd finished.

And when I'd wrapped the silver up and put it away again, there was Frau Muller's parlor to dust and sweep; and then she pretended she'd got to sort through all the last year's menus, and gave me the job of putting them in order—scrappy, dusty, torn things, of no use to anyone. I could see quite plainly what she was doing: keeping me busy, of course, and away from Charlotte. All afternoon she stood over me, while thoughts of Charlotte locked in the tower and Lucy wandering over the mountains on her own, and Miss Davenport close enough to help but quite ignorant of their trouble, went round and round in my head like cats fighting in a bag.

Count Karlstein went out later, with the hounds; which lowered my spirits still further. Then, in the late afternoon, Frau Muller told me to take some logs up to the drawing-room and trim the lamps. I thought this would give me a chance to run up to the lumber room, but again I was thwarted, for I found Herr Snivelwurst snoring sulkily by the ghost of the drawing-room fire and I dropped a heavy pair of tongs on the stone hearth to wake him up with a start.

He jerked and snorted and sat up suddenly, then saw who it was and sank back into the chair again—and then woke up fully.

"Where were you when I fell in the river? I thought you'd gone to get help?"

"I had, sir! I ran and ran! I was so worried about you—"

"I might very easily have drowned, I suppose you realize. I'm a remarkably strong swimmer—many have said how powerfully I swim—but the force of the current was overwhelming. I was near carried to my death—" Here he broke off for a fit of sneezing. I turned away and made as if to leave. "Here, I haven't finished!" he said. "I was going to tell you how I trapped that little minx—you'll enjoy that."

"I'm busy, Herr Snivelwurst," I said. "I expect I'll hear it again."

He sneezed once more and sank back, grumbling. I left.

But then, at last, came the chance I'd been waiting for.

They'd relented; or Frau Muller's stony heart had softened to the extent of allowing that Charlotte might, at least, be fed in her imprisonment, and so Frau Wenzel had prepared a tray with a bowl of soup, some bread, and an apple, and I was to take it—not to the tower, indeed, but to Frau Muller herself, who was presently in the hall on some business and who would take it up to the prisoner. I took the tray and went up the stone steps from the kitchen, while Frau Wenzel clattered away behind me at some pots and pans. The passage to the hall led past Frau Muller's parlor, and there, I knew, hung a full set of duplicate keys for all the rooms in the castle except the count's study.

It only took a moment. I slipped into the room, set the tray on the table, turned to the great board behind the door and ran my eyes feverishly up and down until I saw the key; and then I put it into the bowl. Frau Wenzel's soup was good and thick, thank goodness, and the key was completely hidden.

I picked up the tray again as the door opened, and in came Frau Muller. I stood, frozen. She said nothing, but her eyes glittered with a sly triumph. Without a word she took the tray from me and waited for me to leave the room. "Wait in the hall," she said, with a nasty edge to her voice, and disappeared in the gloom of the stairway.

I stood by the hall fire, crushed with misery. I nearly wept; the only thing that stopped me was the thought of the pleasure she'd take in my tears. After what seemed an age her footsteps came down the stairs again and I turned to face her.

But before she could speak, the main door of the castle was flung open, and Count Karlstein himself, the cold air swirling around him like an army of Visigoths, stood there on the threshold. The wind flung up cinders and ash from the hearth and made the lamplight flare and sink, and even the heavy, sagging tapestries stirred uneasily out from the walls before the count slammed the door, shutting out the wind. Frau Muller was at his side, speaking swiftly, pointing at me. He looked up and his eyes seemed to flicker, like the mountains in summer when a storm's about to break, with enormous undischarged anger.

He took three swift strides, and raised the short stick in his hand to strike at me. I stepped back, but the blow caught me on my shoulder; even through my dress it stung fiercely, and I cried out in fear and scrambled away as he aimed another blow. It cut me across the neck, and I turned and ran. He was mad. He shouted at me—a stream of abuse that turned me cold to hear it—and flung something; I don't know what it was, but it struck me in the back just before I reached the door to the servants' quarters. It was hard and heavy, and the spot was tender for weeks afterward. I flung myself into the kitchen and sobbed and sobbed—and Frau Wenzel, instead of comforting me, turned away, her face tight and shut with fear, and clattered some buckets in the scullery.

And only a moment later the door was flung wide, and there stood Frau Muller, leaning forward and craning her neck at me, white with anger—except for a little broken vein that stretched like a thread of scarlet cotton up the side of her nose. I stared hard at that to avoid looking into her eyes, and she said, "Get your cloak and your bags, and go. Get out! Leave the castle immediately, and don't come back!"

My head was reeling, but I managed to curtsy. I felt as if I was dreaming. She stood aside to let me pass, holding her skirt fastidiously out of the way.

It was the work of a few minutes to gather my possessions; and then, sore, full of fear, and utterly defeated, I left Castle Karlstein as the snow began to fall, and stumbled down the road toward the village.

PART TWO

Narratives by Various Hands

Lucy's Narrative

No, we should never have left the hut. It was Folly. But we were so hungry and so cold that to stay there would have been Madness; and though we were certainly foolish, we were not yet mad. So we left.

The second act of Folly was Charlotte's. I tried to call to her in the voice of some woodland creature, since I was still hidden among the trees and did not wish to reveal my presence; but although I could see quite clearly that the stranded form on the bank was that of Herr Snivelwurst, my bird imitation failed to convey this knowledge to Charlotte, and I watched, squawking dismally, as she walked into the trap and was led off into captivity.

For the rest of the morning and most of the afternoon I haunted the woods, in a state of horrible Indecision, and even more horrible Hunger; until at last, in desperation, I entered the village and made my way to the Jolly Huntsman. Despite Hildi's misgivings, I thought that there would surely be some help to be found in that convivial spot. And so there was; but not of a kind I was expecting.

I entered the parlor and found it deserted. But on a platform at the end stood the strangest object I had ever seen. It was a Cabinet, rather taller and broader than a man, and it was covered with all manner of projections, handles, eyepieces, nozzles, windows, curtains, knobs, and mystic signs. Struck with Curiosity, I wandered up to examine it; and suddenly the curtains were parted and a man appeared.

He was tall, and quite unlike anyone I had seen before. He did not look Swiss at all, but somehow Italian, and he was exceedingly handsome. His eyes glittered disapprovingly as he looked down at me.

"Have you seen my servant?" he said.

"No, sir," I faltered.

"Max!" he called. "Oh, this is impossible. Where is that man? Max!"

He opened the Cabinet and brought out a long robe, covered in the signs of the Zodiac, which he hung over one of the knobs on the door.

"Excuse me, sir—" I began.

"What is it, little girl?"

"Have you seen Hildi, sir?"

"Never heard of her. Hold this." And he handed me a Human Skull. I took it with trembling hands. "Don't drop it," he said. "It is the Skull of Apollonius, the great philosopher. Quite irreplaceable."

"What shall I do with it?"

"Hold it up," he said. "Gaze into its eyes. Look mysterious. Yes! Perfect! Just stand there. Don't move an inch."

"But please—I'm in trouble—can I look for Hildi?"

"Hush, child! You are treading on the edge of Mysteries." He walked around me, scrutinizing me closely. "Yes," he said finally. "You will make a perfect assistant."

Then I nearly did drop the Skull.

"What?" I gasped. "An assistant? What do you mean, sir?"

"You are running away, are you not?"

"Well—yes—but how do you know?"

"Easy to tell. What *you* need is somewhere to hide, and what *I* need is an assistant, since my servant has vanished. What is your name?"

"It's Lucy—but may I hide here? Will you not give me away? I am in great danger, and my sister—"

"Give you away? A scandalous idea! As sure as my name is Dante Cadaverezzi, I shall not betray a fellow fugitive. The Skull, if you please." He replaced Apollonius in the Cabinet, and began to arrange various mysterious articles on the stage nearby.

"Are you running away as well, Mr. Cadaverezzi?" I said, feeling more at ease. He was a daunting figure, but I felt oddly safe with him.

"*Doctor* Cadaverezzi, if you please. Yes, I am a mountebank, a vagabond," he said. "An honorable calling, but an unstable one. Now, what did you say your name was? Lucy? No, that's no good. You'll have to be a princess....From India? Peru? No—I have it. Egypt, of course! And you shall prophesy—you shall tell fortunes!"

"Shall I? What do you mean?"

"For an extra fee they can have their fortunes told by the Magnetized Princess. Have you ever been Magnetized?"

"No, never—"

"Very easy. You close your eyes, I make the mystic passes, and then you open your eyes and look Magnetic. Very easy. Like this!"

I stood as he showed me, and he pretended to Magnetize me. He was right—it was quite simple.

"Now, if you are a princess, you must have a crown and some kind of robe. There! This will do—" He draped a tablecloth around me. "And for the crown—the very coronet of Charlemagne," he said, producing an ancient crown of gold and setting it gently on my head.

"Isn't it very precious?" I said. "I don't want to break it or anything—"

"Extremely precious. But I can easily make another. Yes, you're much better than my servant Max—a very good-hearted fellow, but a booby. If I Magnetized him, he'd fall over and drop the Skull and overturn the Cabinet and put his foot right through the crystal ball, and I don't know what besides. Now let me show you how the Flying Devil works. There is a spring, here, which you must release when I give the signal...."

And I was helpless. For the next two hours I was rehearsed rigorously in all the Mysteries of the Cabinet, until my head was reeling and my arms were aching; and it was only when I could stand up no longer that he allowed me to stop and ordered some food and wine to be brought in. I had not had an opportunity to tell him that I was hungry, somehow; he had a very forceful Character.

He allowed me to rest for ten minutes or so, and

79

then it was back to work. I tried to tell him about Charlotte and the trouble we were in, but although he listened, I could tell that his mind was on the coming performance. He would suddenly leap to his feet and describe an Effect that he had just thought of, and insist that I try it there and then, and repeat it constantly until I had it perfect; and gradually, as the evening (and the performance) drew nearer, I came to realize that I had fallen into the hands of the most disconcerting of all specimens of Humanity, *viz.* the Genius.

Time swept past in a Phantasmagoria of Skulls and crystal balls and Flying Devils and Spiritual Bells and playing cards and the Illusion of the Broken Watch, and more knobs and handles and switches and levers than I would have thought it possible to fit into a single Cabinet, until I began to feel that if I had not been Magnetized before, I was truly Magnetized now; and then the clock on the wall struck the hour of nine—the doctor hastily draped the robe around me, set the crown on my head, whispered a last instruction, thrust me into the Cabinet, and closed the door.

Darkness surrounded me. I could hear the audience assembling. The performance was about to begin.

HILDI'S NARRATIVE

 Since there was no point in even begin-
ning to look for Lucy, I stayed on the road
(for all that the wind tried to blow me off
it) and made my way back to the village
and the warm kitchen of the Jolly
Huntsman. Ma welcomed me, and clucked
and fussed over the weal the count's whip
had made on my neck, and sat me down
with a bowl of soup and some wine, and then turned back
to her work; for she was nearly distracted by busyness.

The inn was full to bursting. The roar of songs, the clatter of dishes, the shouts of laughter, and the calls for food
made the rafters ring. Elise and Hannerl were running in
and out of the kitchen, their arms full of dishes—full one
way, piled high with steaming sausages and cabbage and
mounds of dumplings, and empty the other—dishes that
ended this round tour in the sink, where, before long, I
found myself up to the elbows in hot water. Taking the easy
way out, perhaps, instead of trudging like King Wenceslas

through the snow in the hope of finding some trace of Lucy. But when I'd thought that far, another load of dishes would arrive and be set down perilously on the wet draining-board and I had to start all over again.

What I really wanted, I now realized, was to talk to Peter. Maybe I could manage to get down to the cellar if there was a moment later on....

"Why's it so busy?" I asked Ma, during a rare interval in her rushing from the kitchen to the parlor and back again.

"What? Oh, it's Doctor Cadaverezzi's performance! I thought everyone in the valley had heard about it."

"Oh, yes! I did know—but I'd forgotten. He gave me that poster to put up."

"He thought he'd have to cancel it earlier."

"Why?"

"His servant's disappeared. You don't know the half of it—it's been all go down here. First of all there was that nonsense of Sergeant Snitsch's, with the papers and all— and then Doctor Cadaverezzi lost his servant. He wanted him to help set the Cabinet up—I don't know what he does with it, but, my word, it looks impressive—and he couldn't find the fellow anywhere. And he hasn't turned up yet. But then he found someone else, apparently, and when I came down he said it was all right, he could go on with the performance after all. But he'd need the parlor to himself for the afternoon, to rehearse. And of course I said that was fine, and he just got on with it. A real gentleman. And handsome! Oh, Hildi, if your ma's not here in the morning, it's because she's run off with Doctor Cadaverezzi!"

Well, well, I thought; Ma in love. Of course, she wasn't really, and it was just the excitement of the shooting contest and the novelty of having a performer in the inn and so on; and perhaps she'd had a drop of the Johannisberger wine I saw all frosty in the corner. Certainly she wouldn't have spoken like that if Peter'd been there to guffaw at her. At least she seemed to have stopped worrying about him for a while. But the main thing—I had to keep reminding myself—was Lucy. It was the first question I'd asked when I got to the inn, and the answer had been: no, she hadn't turned up here—no one had seen her. I just had to keep hoping.

Doctor Cadaverezzi's performance was arranged for nine o'clock, and when the great old wooden clock in the parlor ticked and lurched its way round to that time, the air of excitement was so thick you could hardly see through it—though that might have been the smoke from the bright China pipes many of the visitors were smoking. Silent, red-faced men, with an air of huge secret enjoyment, as if they were in on a joke that no one else suspected; men from far away in clothes that looked like costumes from a play; stout, slow-moving men, like elderly bears; brisk, dark-featured men, like monkeys; men who couldn't speak a word of German and who had to point to what they wanted and mime and make faces to explain; men with pale faces from the great forests further north; men with sunburned faces and bright narrow eyes, from the snowy glare of the mountains—all of them come for the shooting contest, of course. And then there were the villagers: the raucous boys, Peter's pals, sharp and easy and full of themselves, flirting with Elise and Hannerl; wide-eyed children at their mothers' skirts; middle-aged men who sipped their wine and talked energetically with their fellows; older men who took great care to settle themselves comfortably in a corner and get their pipes going nicely, reckoning that the height of their present ambitions.

And when all this company had crowded into the parlor—Elise and Hannerl at the back, tea towels flung over one shoulder, arms folded, and an attentive young huntsman beside each of them in case they should need an escort to find their way outside during any interval that Doctor Cadaverezzi might allow for, and finally Ma and me, standing on a table by the streaming window—when all this was ready and the show about to begin, I had the first of two surprises that came my way that night.

Because the parlor door opened, and, preceded by the beaming, sneezing, hand-wiping form of Herr Arturo Snivelwurst, hair pomaded Napoleonically and drippy little nose bright cherry-red, came the dark, glowering figure of my late employer, Count Karlstein. And he looked up at me, standing close enough for me to spit in his eye if I'd cared to, and—bowed! There was a nasty air of ironical triumph about him, as distinctive as the odor of cloves about someone with the toothache. The company fell silent; those who knew him because they did, and those who didn't because something about him told them they ought to.

"Good evening," he said in his rasping voice, that metallic tone that appeared when he was trying to be genial. "I have heard of the wonders of this Doctor Cadaverezzi and I have come to patronize his performance."

Snivelwurst was motioning to some of the audience to move aside, and within a minute or two Count Karlstein, with his sniffling, snuffling, sneezing secretary beside him, was seated and provided with wine.

Then Doctor Cadaverezzi, who must have been watching the whole thing from behind the curtain, began his performance.

First of all, a gong was struck—a mighty, Chinese sound, somehow accompanied by invisible dragons and the fumes of opium. Then the curtains were whisked aside, and there beside the Cabinet, lit by some garish and sinister light, was the doctor himself—bowing suavely and fixing his glittering eyes on, seemingly, everyone at once. There was a burst of applause that he'd done nothing to deserve except stand there and look impressive; but some people are like that—you'd sooner watch *them* clean their boots than anyone else walk a tightrope across a cage of hungry tigers. Magnetism—that's what it is.

He held up his hand, and the applause halted.

"My friends: you have no doubt seen many traveling players—fortune-tellers, threadbare actors pretending to be Harlequin or Julius Caesar or Hamlet—of course you have. Please do not confuse me with people of that sort. I have spent a lifetime in the lonely pursuit of knowledge; I have been privileged to serve many monarchs. I was physician to the Great Mogul in India, I was Privy Councillor to the noble Alfonso, King of Brazil. I have risked my life in exploring distant regions of the earth, where no traveler's foot had been set before. And the fruits of all my researches, the treasures I have spent my life assembling, are here in this mystic Cabinet!"

A gong sounded again; the audience was hushed. "First," said the doctor, "I shall introduce you to my personal attendant from the world of spirits—a devil from Lapland. Springer, to me!" He snapped his fingers. There was a puff of smoke from the Cabinet, a loud whizzing sound, and something small and red and horny and whiskery flew out of one of the apertures in the Cabinet and landed neatly in his hand.

And then there came an interruption.

"Nothing but a doll on a spring!" sneered Count Karlstein. "The man's a fraud!"

One or two of the men in the audience nodded. Doctor Cadaverezzi looked like thunder. I thought he was going to lose them for a moment; they're a hard bunch to please, as many players had found to their cost. But I didn't know Doctor Cadaverezzi. Suddenly a smile of childlike innocence spread over his features, like a bubble of pure delight.

"Next," he said, "I shall show you a trick that has baffled audiences from Paris to Peru. Has anyone got a watch that I may borrow?"

"Yes! Yes!" shouted Count Karlstein. "Use this one!"

Doctor Cadaverezzi pretended to be unwilling, but as no one else offered a watch, he had to take Count Karlstein's.

"You'll see," said the count gleefully as Doctor Cadaverezzi made his way back to the front, "he'll pretend to smash it. I've seen this trick before!"

Doctor Cadaverezzi held up a large red-spotted handkerchief and placed the watch inside it. "Your watch is in here, my lord," he said, wrapping it up.

"Of course it is!" said the count, enjoying himself hugely.

"Now I shall take this very heavy mallet," said the doctor, holding it up, "and smash the watch to pieces."

"Go on, then!" called the count, laughing loudly. "I

know how it's done, Snivelwurst! I've seen Goldini do this. Yes, go on, smash it!"

"With your permission, then," said Doctor Cadaverezzi politely, "I shall strike your watch with the mallet and break it to pieces."

"Go on, go on!" Count Karlstein waved impatiently. Doctor Cadaverezzi put the wrapped-up watch on a small table next to him and struck it several heavy blows with the mallet.

In between the blows, the count was explaining to the audience that the watch wasn't there at all—that it was up Cadaverezzi's sleeve and that he'd shortly produce it from the other side of the room or from someone's hat. Snivelwurst, by this time, was nodding and beaming and rubbing his hands at Cadaverezzi's coming discomfiture; and poor Ma, by my side, was almost beside herself with bitterness at Count Karlstein's spoilsport behavior.

Finally, when the handkerchief had been well and truly battered, Doctor Cadaverezzi almost humbly picked it up and carried it to Count Karlstein, who was now roaring with laughter.

"Your watch, my lord," he said.

"Ha, ha! My watch! You don't think I fell for that, do you?" cried Count Karlstein. He took the handkerchief and held it high, showing it to everyone. "Let's have a look, then," he said, and opened it up. His expression changed as he pulled out a string of cogs, springs, bits of broken glass and bent silver, and a long watch chain. "What's this?" he demanded.

"Your watch, as I explained," said Doctor Cadaverezzi. "I said I was going to smash it, and these ladies and gentlemen will bear witness to the fact that you told me to go ahead and do it."

Murmurs of agreement and nods came from the audience, who didn't like the count.

"But—but—"

"So that is just what I have done." Doctor Cadaverezzi shrugged, with all the melancholy politeness in the world; but a sparkle in his eyes told me, and the rest of the audience, that he'd won this little contest.

And the best was yet to come. As Count Karlstein sat down angrily and turned to Snivelwurst, the doctor produced an identical red handkerchief from somewhere else and took out of it...Count Karlstein's watch! He looked at it with droll pride, slipped it into his breast pocket, and patted it with satisfaction. This little mime took only a second, but the audience saw it and roared with approving laughter—which only annoyed Count Karlstein the more, as he didn't know what they were laughing at.

And so Doctor Cadaverezzi moved on, having captured his audience completely. They all knew, now, that he was a trickster—that if you turned your back on him, he'd pick your pocket; but it didn't seem to matter, as they were all in a high good humor. And he did it so well, with such a delight in his own tricks, that you couldn't help but enjoy it. So now we saw what all the strange knobs and handles and levers on the Cabinet were for: this one, for instance, worked a device called the Chromoeidophusikon, and Hans Pfafferl was shoved up out of the front row by his pals and made to press his face close to the eyepiece while Doctor Cadaverezzi turned a handle and a little windmill on top of the Cabinet revolved, and loud bangs and whizzing sounds and whistles came from inside. Hans was seeing, the doctor assured us, a clockwork representation of the Battle of Bodelheim, with musical, optical, and ballistical effects—and when Hans staggered away from the Cabinet, his face was printed a medley of colors that made him look like a savage from one of the heathen lands Doctor Cadaverezzi claimed to have visited. He didn't understand the laughter at all.

Finally, there came the climax of the show.

The Chinese gong sounded once, twice, three times, and Doctor Cadaverezzi struck an attitude of awe, as if some terrifying supernatural event was about to take place. Indeed, according to him, it was.

"The hour of the Ibis is at hand!" he announced in solemn tones. "As prophesied in the ancient almanacs, we are about to witness the rebirth of that sacred princess known to the high priests as Nephthys! She has slumbered in the pyramids for ten thousand years—but tonight she shall rise and speak to us in the hieroglyphics of her native tongue. Ladies and gentlemen—the princess Nephthys!"

Some strange chords were sounded on a muffled harp and a cloud of smoke rolled out of the Cabinet; and from out of the smoke, robed in white and with a diadem of gold on her brow, her hands folded across her breast and her eyes cast mystically upward, stepped my second surprise of the night: Lucy.

So she *had* come here! And—

In a second or so, Count Karlstein—he'd already risen from his chair—would have her in his grasp. There was only one thing to do.

"Fire! Fire!" I shouted, and jumped down and flung the door wide. "Help! Fire! Fire!"

It worked. Within a moment, the whole parlor was in an uproar. Those at the back looked around nervously, those at the front struggled to push their way to the back, those in the middle were caught uncertainly between the two of them. And I stood outside, banging two trays together and yelling at the top of my voice. Soon the door was jammed, and arms and legs and roaring heads were all flailing this way and that, trying to get out.

But in the second or so after I'd shouted, I'd seen Lucy open her eyes, startled, and look first at me and then, horrified, at Count Karlstein. What Doctor Cadaverezzi was doing, I had no idea, but Count Karlstein and Snivelwurst were struggling against the press of people, trying to reach the front of the parlor while everyone else was making for the back. I hoped—for I couldn't see—that Lucy would have the time and the sense to get away.

But meanwhile the people who'd been in the parlor were milling around and shouting, calling for buckets of water, for blankets to stifle the flames, and for axes to chop down doors and let out anyone behind them; and some were yelling to others to open all the windows wide to let out the smoke, and others were yelling even louder not to, since it'd let in a draft to fan the flames—and not a single person realized that there was no fire at all. I didn't like it. It was disturbing to see that cheerful, lively audience turn in a moment into a confused mob. I slipped through the middle of them and into the kitchen. There was a back way out, through the scullery and the outhouse, and I stumbled through, banging my legs on buckets and crates and making, I daresay, a lot of noise. I hoped Peter wouldn't hear and poke his silly head out of the cellar to see what was going on.

There is a narrow alley behind the Jolly Huntsman, and as I reached it, I was just in time to see, disappearing out of the other end of it, the form of a tall man with a cloak and a large hat. Doctor Cadaverezzi! I set off after him, not daring to call his name in case Count Karlstein had found his way out and was nearby. He'd be after Cadaverezzi, too, now. I reached the other end of the alley, which opened out into the road that led down to the bridge, and looked around, breathless.

He was nowhere to be seen. Behind me, I could hear a commotion from the tavern—angry shouts that I didn't like the sound of. The road and the bridge were empty, gleaming white in the moonlight; and the river ran swiftly past, glinting and throwing up little liquid sparks of silvery light, and not helping a bit. I peered hard into the darkness beyond the river, where the trees began and the road curved up around the mountain. Was that a movement among the tree trunks? It was too dark, and too far off. The forest was full of shadows. And on this side of the river—just the village, the snow-covered roofs, the muddy road, the yellow lights in the windows, the smoke from the chimneys rising straight up, thick and white, into the clear bitter air.

I'd lost them.

I turned slowly back to the Jolly Huntsman, shivering with the bone-jarring cold, and weary with despair. Doctor Cadaverezzi, I thought, you'd better look after her. You're all she's got now. And then I thought: if all she's got to save her from Count Karlstein and the Demon Huntsman is a traveling swindler wanted by the police—poor Lucy. Poor Lucy!

Police Report Number 354/21

Subject: EVENTS AT KARLSTEIN POLICE

STATION FOLLOWING THE ARREST OF

THE CABINET OF DOCTOR CARADARISTI

I wish it to be placed on record at the very start of this report that I, that is me, Josef Snitsch, Police Sergeant, holder of the Cadets' Neatness and Smart Turn-Out Award (2nd Class), officer in charge of the Police Station at Karlstein, told my constable, Alphonse Winkelburg, Police Constable, that there was to be no eating on duty.

I told him most particular about this, as I have had trouble with this constable in the past. There was an occasion when he was unable to draw his truncheon with the maximum effectiveness, as laid down in the Police Handbook, due to the presence of a meat pie in the operative hand; and the felon we was attempting to apprehend on that occasion got away scot-free.

So I said to the aforesaid constable before I left the guardroom that he was to be stern and vigilant, and not to let a crumb pass his lips, due to the Cabinet of Wonders what he had to guard.

The aforesaid Cabinet was took into custody following the disappearance of its owner, a Doctor Crackanutsi, an Italian. The aforesaid Doctor Catchanitsi had vanished under suspicious circumstances following the false alarm of a fire at the Jolly Huntsman. His Cabinet was arrested instead, him not being there to arrest, and held in the Police Station pending further developments.

This was a dangerous mission for Constable Winkelburg, him not being very swift either in wind or limb and the Cabinet being furnished with all manner of foreign devices and articles of a suspicious nature, rendering it highly risky to touch it. While we was conveying it to the Police Station, Constable Winkelburg accidentally touched a hidden spring what released an unexpected jet of ink what I was not expecting and so was unable to avoid. Some rowdy bystanders had to be severely reprimanded for appearing to find this amusing.

The aforesaid ink having rendered my face temporarily unsuitable for the efficient performance of my duties as laid down in the Police Handbook, I left Constable Winkelburg on guard, as described above, warning him sternly against eating on duty, and removed myself to the washroom of the Police Station in order to remove the ink by which I had been defaced. Before going out, however, I removed my helmet and placed it in the bracket designed to hold it. (This bracket is my own design. Drawing enclosed.* It is my belief that, if adopted, this bracket would increase the efficiency of the Police Force one hundredfold. The principle is simple. By placing all unattended business in the upturned helmet the owner is unable to wear it until dealt with. I bring this to the attention of the Authorities not in the hope of profit but in the interests of efficiency.)

Finding that a quantity of the offending ink had soaked into my whiskers, I was some little time in the washroom, and when I emerged, I found Constable Winkelburg in an attitude of guilt, attempting to conceal a paper bag about his person and bearing evi-

[* Drawing now missing.]

dence of the recent consumption of cheesecake upon his chin. I reprimanded him severely, and, being in a state of indignation, did not investigate the inside of my helmet before placing it firmly upon my head. It was then that I discovered that Constable Winkelburg, hearing my approach, had dropped the larger uneaten portion of his cheesecake into the helmet.

It is my hope that this introductory preamble will explain my unpolicelike bearing and undignified appearance at the time of the arrest.

I now come to the events what followed.

Knowing the habits of felons, I was able to predict that the criminal in question, Doctor Calamatipsy, would attempt to regain possession of the Cabinet of Wonders, and so I ordered Constable Winkelburg to hide in the guardroom with the lamp turned out, in a state of darkness. I, meanwhile, concealed myself in an adjacent cupboard, with my truncheon drawn in readiness.

Several hours appeared to pass.

Eventually our vigil was rewarded.

Using a key of some ingenious or foreign manufacture, the villain aforesaid, Doctor Canackadesky, inserted himself through the portals of the Police Station. As described above, I was expecting him, due to my knowledge of the felonious mind, but I was not expecting him to be accompanied by a female of tender years.

I transcribe their conversation exactly. I am able to do so with perfect confidence, being as how I gained the Ernst Stuffelbaum Plate for Memory Training in the Police Academy.

Their words was as follows:

SHE: I am surprised at you, Doctor
Calackabitsy, being as how I thought you
was honest.
HE: Oh, I am as honest as the day is long.
SHE: But this is winter and the days are
very short.
HE: That is why I am less honest in the winter than in the summer. Now let us just
retrieve my Cabinet and then we can retreat
to some place of safety at a convenient distance.

SHE: But, Doctor, I seen you with my own eyes. I have no alternative but to reprimand you severely. When that man was bending over applying his eyes to the eyepiece and I dabbed his face with all paint like what you said while all them cannons was going off and that, I seen you pick his pocket. You cannot deny it.

HE: Indeed I cannot. I have his wallet here, I am glad to say.

SHE: Then that is very wicked of you.

HE: The public is a very nervous and shy creature. It has to be helped to invest in magnificent enterprises like the Cabinet of Wonders.

SHE: You must not excuse your stealing by calling it helping your victims to invest. I am very grateful to you for helping me, but you are wicked and dishonest. I would never of agreed to help you if I had have known that it would lead me into enterprises of a felonious nature.

HE: Very wise. Now let us retrieve my

Cabinet while these two policemen are temporarily vacating the premises.

SHE: And then will you help me rescue Charlotte?

HE: Yes. Now hold the lantern high while I attempt to lift the Cabinet.

At that point, deeming it an appropriate moment, I sprang out from my place of concealment in order to apprehend the villain. Unfortunately, while concealing myself I had overlooked the presence of a bucket in the cupboard and had inserted my left foot therein, what got in the way of my springing out and caused me to fall heavily and dent my helmet.

When I had recovered my composure, I addressed the villain.

"Doctor Crackawhipsy," I announced, "I arrest you in the name of the law."

To my astonishment I saw that the person in question was not Doctor Caramolesty at all, but an agent of the Venetian Secret Service, posing under an alias. He greeted me by name. I was temporarily unsure of the correct procedure, being as how the Police

Handbook does not cover cases like this, when I caught sight of the recumbent boots of Constable Winkelburg. It seemed as how he had fallen asleep while on duty. I could hardly believe my eyes. I woke him up and reprimanded him severely, and under the distraction afforded by this I was able to rapidly and swiftly evaluate the situation.

Using my Police training, I was able to come to the conclusion that the Venetian secret agent and Doctor Canalarresty were one and the same person, and that one of them was masquerading as the other, contrary to the law. I had no alternative but to apply the full rigor of the powers at my disposal.

I said to the aforesaid villain that I was arresting him, and began to caution him in the manner laid down in the Police Handbook.

He then said the following words:

"Lucy, blow the lantern out."

The young female person treacherously did so, plunging the entire Police Station into a state of darkness. Calling to Constable Winkelburg to come to my aid, I leapt fearlessly forward and grappled with the miscreant, receiving several heavy blows but succeeding after a fierce struggle in subduing him and applying the Police Handcuffs, in the manner laid down in the Police Handbook.

I called in an authoritative way for the lamp to be re-lit.

When this was done, I found to my dismay that I had arrested Constable Winkelburg, that he had simultaneously arrested me, and that we were now inextricably linked by means of the aforesaid handcuffs. Doctor Caracapesty then made several observations of an opprobrious and offensive nature.

Having done that, he and his accomplice were about to withdraw with their Cabinet when the door of the Police Station was flung open and there entered a squad of reinforcements from the Geneva Police, under the command of Inspector Hinkelbein.

Inspector Hinkelbein expressed his surprise at finding Constable Winkelburg and myself trussed up in an undignified and unpolicelike manner. I attempted to explain the reasons for it, but he cut me short. This is the first opportunity I have had of clearing my name.

The inspector then arrested Doctor Caravelupsy,

accusing him of being Luigi Brilliantini, the well-known confidence trickster. It was clear to me that the inspector had made an error of identification, and I was about to explain it to him when he cut me short.

Constable Winkelburg then drew the inspector's attention to the fact that the girl had disappeared during the fracas. The inspector expressed his surprise that two grown officers of the Police Force should be beaten by one little girl. I attempted to correct his interpretation of the facts, but he cut me short.

The prisoner was then conveyed to the cells. Constable Winkelburg and myself was released from our handcuffs and severely reprimanded. I then informed Inspector Hinkelbein that he could expect to receive the Order of the Golden Banana, but he mistook my meaning. I tried to explain, but he cut me short.

The prisoner, Doctor Caravanipsky, is at present under guard in the Police Station, awaiting transit to Geneva, there to answer charges of impersonation.

(Signed)

Josef Sritsch

Police Sergeant

Miss Augusta Davenport's Narrative

After I left Castle Karlstein, I must confess I felt a trifle disconcerted; and that was a feeling I had not experienced since being surrounded by savage tribesmen in the wilds of Turkestan.

However, then, as now, I was able to console myself with the reflection that an English gentlewoman can rise above any circumstances, given intelligence and a loaded pistol. Both of those properties I had, and, tucking the latter into my muff, I set off to find some quiet spot in which to exercise the former.

Very soon I found a deserted graveyard overlooking a rocky gorge. It was an admirable place; not only did it command an extensive view of some very fine geological formations, but it also had that gloomy air which invariably leads superstitious persons to declare such a place haunted and avoid it. And solitude was exactly what I wanted.

Later in the afternoon, however, I began to regret the action of that very foolish policeman in banning me from the village, since it made it necessary to camp. Fortunately I had my very useful *Hermes* patent folding cart with me, containing every necessity for survival; and, when I had come to certain conclusions regarding Count Karlstein, I set off down the road toward the forest, where I was sure, I thought, of finding some secluded glade in which to pitch my tent. I was very sorry that my maid Eliza had not been able to find me. She has a practical nature (which is good) and a warm heart (which is better) but a soft head (which is no good at all). She would be no more capable of walking alone up a deserted road toward a darkened graveyard, haunted or not, than of using the differential calculus. I would not ask her to. Nevertheless, I regretted her absence.

Judge of my surprise, then, when I rounded a bend in the road and encountered the girl herself. She was deep in conversation with a young man, evidently a servant of some kind, whose face seemed somehow familiar to me. I hailed her.

"Oh! Miss Davenport! Thank goodness you're safe! Thank goodness we've found you!" she exclaimed.

I refrained from pointing out that it was I who had found her, and told her what had happened at the castle. She clasped her hands in horror.

"Oh, the wickedness!" she cried. "If only we'd known, we'd never have agreed to look for them! Oh, the monster of deceit and treachery—" and so on. I had no idea what she was talking about; I let her ramble for a moment or so, while I examined the young man.

"Have I not seen you before?" I inquired.

"I took the liberty of accompanying your maid, ma'am, so as to protect her in these wild regions," he said. "I have had the honor of serving you before, as it happens. I was a coachman, ma'am, and I drove you into Geneva, which was where I had the pleasure of meeting Miss Eliza here."

A smart, well-spoken, polite young man. I approved. It was plain, even in the twilight, that the two of them were in love.

"What is your name?"

"Max Grindoff, ma'am, at your service."

"And you are a coachman, you say?"

"Not anymore, ma'am. I'm the gentleman's personal attendant and lackey in chief to the great Doctor Cadaverezzi, who owns the Cabinet of Wonders, ma'am."

"Hmm. I see. Now, Eliza, you said something just now about *looking for them*. To whom were you referring?"

"The little girls, miss! Charlotte and Lucy!"

"Explain."

She did so. As she spoke, Count Karlstein's plan—though not, of course, the reasons for it yet—began to reveal itself to me. He had treated the girls in such a manner that they had run away; he had concealed the fact by telling me a pack of lies about their being ill; and now he was trying to recapture them.

"I shall have to see to this," I said. "Now, Grindoff, my man. You have been looking for these girls since this morning, I take it?"

"Well, ma'am..." He shuffled his feet.

"But with no success, evidently."

"None at all, ma'am. But this forest is remarkable large and they might be anywhere. They might even have gone over the mountains into the next valley or beyond, ma'am. They could be in Italy—"

"Stuff and nonsense. They won't be far away. No, there's only one thing to do. Count Karlstein knows of my interest—he won't be taken in by a second visit from me. But he doesn't know you. You'll have to go up to the castle."

"What, me, ma'am? What for, if you don't mind my asking?"

"To find out why they ran away in the first place. Ask the servants. Introduce yourself into the kitchen. I'm sure you can manage that."

"But my master, ma'am," he said, "he'll be expecting me back at the Jolly Huntsman any minute now. He's got a show to perform tonight."

"Well, if you hurry, you could be there and back before he begins."

"You'll have to leave your trombone with us, Maxie," said Eliza.

"It ain't a trombone, Eliza, it's a coach-horn," he said.

I looked at it—a long, straight brass instrument. I asked to examine it more closely and he handed it to me.

"I saw a South American blowpipe once," I told them, "in Signor Rolipolio's Exhibition at Clarence Gardens. It very much resembled this. Signor Rolipolio himself was kind enough to demonstrate the art of firing them....Allow me."

Among the provisions I always carry, a bag of dried peas holds an honored place. I extracted one now, placed it in the mouthpiece of the coach-horn, and took aim at a nearby sapling. The pea flew out and struck the slender trunk full in the center.

"Well, I've never seen that done before," said

Grindoff. "That's a good trick, that is. My master'd like to use it in his act, I've no doubt."

"Oh, Maxie! Do be careful!" said Eliza. "Don't you get caught by the count and locked in the cellars, will you, my love?"

"Well, I, er…"

"Eliza," I said, "you must assist me in finding somewhere to camp. We shall meet Mr. Grindoff, when he returns, in some convenient place."

"We saw a woodcutter's hut, miss, just a little way back," she said. "It's all broken down, but we could put up your tent easy enough. And there's water from the stream nearby. We'll see you there, Maxie, my love. All right?"

He opened and shut his mouth once or twice, but evidently the force of his affection for her had rendered him incapable of resistance. He nodded sadly and trudged up the road toward the castle.

"An excellent young man, Eliza," I said.

"I must confess I fell in love with him in Geneva, miss," she said, "when I seen him on the coach, all proud, with his harness jingling and his uniform all smart and his trombone glittering in the sun…."

"Yes, yes, I understand, my dear. I am not a stranger to the noble passion. Signor Rolipolio quite stole my heart three years ago….But it was not to be. Fate parted us."

"Oh, dear, miss," she said, deeply sympathetic. Anything with a hint of romance in it melted her heart at once—poor simple girl. "How sad for you. And him too. I bet he's pining his heart away in a foreign land...."

"No doubt, no doubt. He is the only man, Eliza, who was my equal in point of character, audacity, and intellect. But some foolish trouble over passports or papers meant that he had to leave the country, and I fear that there was some political trouble with the government of his native land....Ah well, let us put these melancholy thoughts aside. Duty calls!"

So saying, I accompanied her along the road to the woodcutter's hut and our prospective campsite.

Charlotte's Narrative

When that deceitful man, Herr Snivelwurst, seized my wrist with his wet hand, I felt quite faint with Dismay. But, locked in the lumber room below my uncle's study, some Sternness of Purpose began to return to my Soul.

After all, now I was a captive. And had I not read, only the week before, of the ordeals and the triumph of *Marianna, the Captive of the Abruzzi*? She was imprisoned by her wicked cousin in order to force her to make over her fortune to him. A strangely similar plight to mine! Yet it was not

my fortune (for I had none) which was at stake, but my Life; and while Marianna had friends and a lover, Verocchio, who fought for her release, I had no one. Except for Hildi, of course.

I sat down, as the key turned in the lock and my Imprisonment began, and refused to acknowledge the Tears that coursed as free as the mountain torrents down my cheeks. I sat, in fact, as if I were a Princess defying her executioners—with a straight back and my hands folded in my lap and my head held high; and I blessed the memory of dear Miss Davenport, and her insistence that young ladies should comport themselves with Great Dignity even under the most Trying Circumstances.

I comported myself thus for about a minute, and then I could bear it no longer and lay down and cried properly.

It was a Horrid room. The window had not been cleaned since the invention of glass, and, besides, was barred with rusty iron rods set deeply into the stone. The bare floor was covered in dust; and such a jumble of objects filled the place as had never, I daresay, been seen since before the Flood.

Being thoroughly cold and tired, I tried to sleep. There was a large tapestry draped over the back of a broken-down couch, and I might have covered myself with it for warmth had it not been for the picture it showed—a female Saint, I think, undergoing Circumstances even more Trying than mine—which made me extremely uneasy. So I bundled it up and thrust it out of sight behind an oak cabinet, and lay and shivered for a long time.

But I could not sleep. I might have occupied my mind usefully with Improving Thoughts, but the only Improvement I could imagine then was a pair of wings, to enable me to fly to freedom. And, of course, a Head for Heights. I cleared the dust from the window and peered out hopefully, but there was nothing but a Horrid Precipice, with jagged crags several thousands of feet below.

Was there anything, I wondered (in the spirit of Marianna, the Captive of the Abruzzi), in the room itself with which I could effect an escape? Marianna had spent her time reflecting upon her situation and drawing Moral Conclusions, but then she, poor girl, had been shut in a chilly dungeon, and chained, besides, so there was not a great deal for her to look at. I supposed that I would need some kind of Implement with which to prize open the door. But the only Implements at hand seemed to be made of porcelain. One was a shepherdess and the other was a dog, and they were both broken. I searched further and found: a bent telescope; a glass paperweight; a statue of some Indian god, dented; a box containing specimens of dead butterflies, pinned to a board; a chipped decanter with a sticky little puddle of something sweet in the bottom. (I tasted it—it was too sweet, and just as I sipped, I thought of Poison and nearly choked.) There were several old dresses, very dusty, full of moths; a broken looking-glass; a portrait of a fat lady; a portrait of a fat boy and girl, both very disagreeable, and a fat dog, even more so; a dull Dutch-looking landscape, in oil, without a frame; a dull peeling-gilt frame, of a different size, without a picture; a gentleman's full-bottomed wig, inhabited by moths, the cousins of those in the dresses—the male branch of the family, no doubt; and—Horrid Discovery!—a Human Head.

I have no doubt that I shrieked and put my hands to my mouth. I have observed that that is what I do when I am Startled. But the head that had startled me wore a good-humored, jolly expression and seemed not at all put out to have lost the company of its body.

It was, of course, made of wood. I realized that it belonged to the wig. It had a little pedestal and a brightly painted face and was altogether the cheerfulest object that I had seen for many months; and I was so lonely by then that I spoke to it and set it up on the bamboo table beside the ottoman, and shook its wig for it and dressed it again. And instantly I felt more cheerful, as if I had been visited by a jovial old soul whose only purpose was to look after me.

I told him everything that had happened and he listened with wonderful patience. And then, as if he were bringing me luck, I heard footsteps coming up the stairs. The key turned in the lock.

It was Frau Muller. I sat in a Dignified Manner upon the ottoman and looked straight ahead of me. She said nothing. I said nothing. She set down a tray upon the bamboo table and turned to leave. She left. She locked the door. She went downstairs.

Food!

There was a bowl of Frau Wenzel's thickest soup, two slices of bread, an apple, and a glass of water. I ate ravenously and quite without manners; I even spoke with my mouth full. To the wooden man, of course. He didn't mind.

But I had not finished the soup before I made an Astonishing Discovery. Something hard clinked as I dipped my spoon into the bowl; I pushed it to the side—it fell back into the soup, but not before I had seen that it was a key! With the help of a slice of bread, I got it out and sucked it dry. Hildi—no one else could have done it! I blessed her, and I blessed Herr Woodenkopf, too, for the luck he'd brought.

Being Prudent, I finished the soup before I escaped. (No sense in wasting it.) Being trained by Miss Davenport to anticipate emergencies, I refrained from eating the bread and the apple, dried (on a corner of one of the old dresses) the bread I had fished the key out of the soup with, and put bread and apple into my pocket for later. Then, as there was nothing to keep me there any longer, I left.

But it was not as easy as that. I thought that I had better take something warm or else I should freeze to death in the forest, so I wrapped the thickest of the dresses around me. And I could not—though from a Practical Point of View, I knew I should—leave Herr Woodenkopf. He had brought `me luck. And he cheered me up. And if everything else failed, I could at least throw him at Uncle Heinrich. So I picked him up, complete with wig, and we unlocked the door—very quietly; listened—very carefully; shut the door behind us—very nervously; and went downstairs.

It was the longest walk of my life.

Uncle Heinrich's study was upstairs, and he or Herr Snivelwurst might come up or down at any minute; Frau Muller might come up to retrieve the tray; any of the other servants might cross the hall. I reached the stone archway at the bottom, and my heart was beating at least as loudly as the drum of the Red Indians in *Martha, or The Maid of the Woods.* I could hear it very clearly. Herr Woodenkopf, who was pressed against my chest with his wig over one eye, could hear it more clearly still, but that did not stop him protecting me, for the hall was empty. The fire was blazing, but otherwise it was dark.

I was putting it off; but sooner or later I would

have to cross the hall. When I had summoned all my courage, I ran as fast as I could, like a mouse, for the great door, praying to Herr Woodenkopf that it was not locked—and found it open—and sped through—and through the courtyard, and the gateway, and down the road like the very wind.

Oh! It was cold! The dress I'd selected from those mothy bundles blew out clumsily and got in my way, but I blessed its thickness. I fell three times and rolled over and over and got up straight away and ran on. There had been no fall of snow in the last few hours, so I was able to keep to the tracks that had already been made. A little more than halfway down toward the village, I stopped to catch my breath.

And saw, further down the slope but moving unmistakably up toward me, a Man!

I plunged off the road instantly and concealed myself until he had passed. I did not know him, and although it was difficult to see clearly, I thought he looked friendly. But if he was going to the castle, I wanted nothing to do with him. I hardly dared breathe until he was out of sight; and when I moved on I walked and did not run. I did a great deal of shivering and my teeth chattered so much that I put a piece of my bread between them to stop them making so much noise. But they ate it without thinking. They ate the next piece too, and the one after that.

If any of my readers have been Fugitives (and I hope they have not), they will know the way in which every bush, tree, rock, cave, and shadow seems to conceal an enemy eager to pounce. And how a thousand evil spirits perch among the twigs like wicked birds, their little glassy eyes all staring, staring. And how that small black shape ahead of them, so still, so sinister, so intent upon unspeakable evil, mesmerizes them and drains all the strength out of them; how the hood over its head conceals a face of such Horrid Ugliness and Inhuman Malevolence that words cannot describe it; how, when it moves toward you, with a ghoulish enjoyment of the fear it's causing you, and raises its thin arms (is it a Skeleton?) and breaks into a run, uttering little cries of triumph—how, when that happens, you can't help but run yourself, uttering cries of quite another sort.

But when that Ghastly Phantom calls your name, and cries "Stop!" and has the voice of your sister Lucy…

I turned, hardly daring to believe it. And yet it was true.

"Lucy!"

"Charlotte!"

"It isn't you—it's a spirit—"

"What happened? Where've you been?"

"Hush, hush! The woods are full of evil spirits—"

"But where—"

"What—"

"How—"

"When—"

And so on, in the course of which she ate the rest of my bread and we shared the apple, and Herr Woodenkopf sat between us and watched the road to make sure no one was coming.

After she'd run away from the police station, she hadn't known what to do. She'd wandered through the village, not daring to knock on anyone's door in case they turned her in to Sergeant Snitsch—or Uncle Heinrich. So finally, giving up all hope of shelter, she'd turned toward the forest, meaning to find her way to the mountain guide's hut (such a safe refuge it seemed now, to both of us! Snug and warm and dry, and far,

far away; what fools we were to leave it!), only to find herself face to face, on the dark road, with a Frightful Specter dressed in trailing antique robes, and (horror of horrors!) carrying its own head beneath its arm....

How she hadn't turned and run, neither of us knew. But now that she'd made the acquaintance of Herr Woodenkopf, she was quite willing to agree that he wasn't in the least ghastly—and he had the great advantage of not requiring to be fed.

"But we'll have to go up to the hut again," she said. "It's the only safe place. We've just got to get through tomorrow, and then it'll be too late for him to take us to the hunting lodge, because Zamiel will have come and gone—"

"Hush! Don't say his name! I'm sure it's unlucky."

"Well, anyway, we've only got to hide for one more day."

"And night. The night's the most important part."

"Yes—a day and a night," she said impatiently, pushing her way through the snow-laden bushes that grew beside the road. "I'm sure the stream's here somewhere. We'll come across it soon."

I followed, clutching Herr Woodenkopf tightly.

"But, Lucy," I said, trying to catch her up, "we can't ever go back, not really."

"Of course we can," she said. But she sounded uncertain.

"Just think what he'll do! There'll be nothing to stop him. He'll be so angry....Oh, Lucy, I don't ever want to go back. I want to go away completely for ever."

She stopped. "I think I do, too," she said. "All right. Let's. We'll go right over the mountains into the next valley and then—just keep going."

The Prospect of Liberty was so delightful that, for a short while, I even forgot the cold. And so, Orphaned Fugitives, we set out through the forest toward Freedom—or toward Death....

Max Grindoff's Narrative

Not being very handy with the pen, I am speaking this to a certain young person who is writing it down for me. I have to set my thoughts in order. This is very difficult. When I was arrested in Geneva for not wearing britches, though that was not my fault, I had a similar difficulty. I am a convivial man, fond of a glass of beer and a smoke and a yarn, and reckoned a capital teller of tall stories — *Strange Passengers I Have Known, The Spook of the Brenner Pass, The Drunk Nun, My Experiences in the Regiment,* all that kind of thing. But when I was sat down in a chilly cell, with chains around my ankles, and made to spin out the

123

tale of my unhappy mishap with the sausages and the drinking-trough to an old person with a squint and a sniff who had to set them all down for the benefit of the court, I found it very trying. Likewise now. As it is, the young person has just told me to get on with it and stop wasting time. But I should like to know, how do you start? It seems to me that a story needs winding up a bit, like a clock, to set it going properly.

I'll start again. Try this:

I have a great admiration for Miss Davenport. She is a lady of great force and spirit. But being so forceful of character — her, I mean — I was not able to reason with her and convince her that it was not a good idea for me to go up to the castle.

It wasn't a good idea because I am not very skillful at jobs like that which require a smooth tongue and an artful manner. My master, Doctor Cadaverezzi, he'd have done it — he was as artful as a bottle of goblins. I remember how he got out of jail, when we became acquainted. I never saw anything like it in my life. What he did was —

The young person is very stern. I have to get on, she says.

Like I should have done then. But didn't, on account

of the idea I had, when I'd gone a little way up the road toward the castle.

That idea was simply to turn around, go back to the village, and tell him about it. I knew what he'd do. He'd raise his eyebrows, as if to say: What? A little matter like that? Nothing could be easier! Then he'd set his hand to his chin, and frown, and say: "But there are certain complications that make it interesting." Then he'd dismiss me and go off to think about it while I'd go and have a yarn in the taproom or polish the Cabinet or mend the Flying Devil (and he was an artful little perisher if ever I saw one. He had a spring up his posterior that was held in by a catch, and he leapt out of the Cabinet like a firework. But he had a mind of his own, that little…I remember once in Basle, we was performing—)

Oh, very well. Where was I?

Looking for the doctor, that's right.

So I turned round and went back to the village—and what did I find? An uproar! A riot! Shouts of *Fire,* and crowds milling about the streets outside the Jolly Huntsman. Not that they're streets like they understand the meaning of the word in Basle, or Geneva. In Geneva, when you say "street," you mean street. Here, they said "street," and they meant lane or track. So I latched on to a fellow from the inn, a useful sort of man with a full bottle in his hand, and asked him what had happened. I wasn't exactly worried, you see, about Doctor Cadaverezzi, because he'd have been able to escape from Noah's Flood itself if he'd had a mind to; but all the same…

"You oughter bin there!" says this fellow. "The Devil hisself come up out the floor!"

"Go on," says I, eyeing his bottle.

"All smoke and sulfur, all springs and horns and whiskers — and that little girl what stood there in the middle of it, a Princess, she was! You oughter seen it!"

A Princess? I thought to myself. He never had no Princess in the Cabinet when I last saw it.

And a fat little lad with a feather in his hat nods solemnly and says, "Oh, yes, I seen him, I seen the Devil, he was there all right, beckoning to Doctor Cadaverezzi with a long sharp finger — and then a trapdoor opened in the floor — I seen it — and all red light and smoke poured up out of it — and the Devil carried Doctor Cadaverezzi and the Princess off to Hell, laughing fit to bust — "

"But what about this fire?" I said.

"The whole place was blazing!" says the little fat lad.

"No, it weren't," says a thin mournful fellow dressed in green. "It were only smoke."

"It were the smoke of Hell itself," says the man with the bottle....

And so on. They're like children, these country folk. I could see I wasn't going to get anywhere with this lot, all contradicting each other and starting off another rumor as soon as they'd managed to swallow the last one.

But the big question was, where was the doctor?

Because no one had seen him at all since the first yell of *Fire*. He'd vanished — and so had that Princess, whoever she was, who kept coming into all the different stories I heard.

We'd moved back inside now and I was snug by the fire in the Jolly Huntsman, with a mug of beer and half a dozen sausages in front of me (but I made sure they stayed on the plate this time — till I ate 'em, of course). And now there was a sensible-looking fellow saying how he saw *her*, the Princess, that is, trying to get away from some little oily fellow who'd got ahold of her — and how he didn't like the look of him, I mean the sensible-looking fellow didn't like the look of the oily-looking fellow, so he spilled a mug of beer down his neck for him and made him let go.

"Good for you," says I. "That was a noble action, giving up your beer like that."

"*My* beer?" says he. "Get away — I wouldn't spill my beer. I got hold of my neighbor's and used that."

I said he was a sensible-looking fellow.

But that set me thinking, that little episode. A Princess, appeared from nowhere — and a missing little girl (well, two, but one'll do for the moment). An uncle, eager to get her back for some dark deed he had in mind — and an oily-looking fellow grabbing hold of the Princess.

Could this oily-looking fellow be the uncle? I never had an uncle, so I couldn't speak from personal experience, but from observing the uncles of others, I reckoned there was two kinds: fat jolly ones and thin old mean ones. I never heard of an oily uncle — it isn't right somehow. But all the same, suppose this Princess had been one of those little girls?

Oh, I'm not a fool, you know. I'm no cuckoo.

So — if the Princess had been here a little while ago, she couldn't be far away now.

128

So—look for a Princess, and I might find a missing girl.

Or—look for the doctor, and I might find the Princess.

Or—look for the missing girl, and I might find the doctor.

Simple!

I finished my sausages and beer and set out. And blow me down if within the next five minutes I didn't come across two scoundrels who had the same idea as I did.

Just in front of the village green there's a big house that belongs to the Mayor. One of those handsome old places, all carved wood and big wide eaves, and what was more, there was a light in one of the windows. This light shone out into his front garden and lit up a bit of the house next door. Between the two houses there was a narrow little alley, and from where I was standing on the bridge, shivering and wondering whether it might be worth having a scout around over the other side of the river, I could see a movement down that alley.

It looked as if someone had just slipped into it, quietly—just the tail end of a movement, like that. There he is! I thought. That's the doctor all right. So I went after him. But I kept quiet, all the same. I've got a police record now; if you're a known criminal, even if it's just a matter of missing britches, you'd better not get caught or else it's the maximum sentence and no arguing. So I went very quietly — and it's a good thing I did.

I got to the Mayor's garden and I was about to turn in to the alley when I heard whispering. It was a still night — you couldn't mistake it. And it wasn't Cadaverezzi at all.

I lowered myself with great care behind a bush, and listened. What I heard was this:

The first bloke said, "I never saw such a fool in my life. All you had to do was hold on to her — you had her in your hand, and you let go!"

The second bloke said, "I'm sorry, Count Karlstein, sir, I deeply and truly and humbly beg your pardon, sir, but — " (then he sneezed) — "but someone tipped a mug of beer down my back, sir, and — " (another sneeze) — "and as I have already suffered one drowning today, sir, my mind was momentarily filled with panic at the thought of another one, and I let go of the girl purely in order to preserve my life — an instinctive reaction, your grace, purely instinctive, quite uncontrollable."

So this was the oily-looking fellow from the Jolly Huntsman that the sensible-looking fellow had told me about! And the other one—he'd called him Count Karlstein! My ears were straining so hard to listen, they must have looked as if they were on tiptoe.

"We'll have to get her back, Snivelwurst," said the first bloke. "And, by the devil himself, if you have her in your hand again, you'd better not let her go, not even if an avalanche descends down your neck. D'you understand?"

"Oh, yes! Yes, indeed! Yes, your grace, that's—" (sneeze)—"very plain indeed, my lord. But, begging your pardon, your grace—" (sneeze)—"we've got one of them back, haven't we? So why, if you don't mind my asking, do we need the second one back, if I may make so bold as to ask?"

"Because if I know anything about Zamiel, he won't be satisfied with one. He'll want a square meal, not a snack. One adult might do—but one small girl wouldn't be enough. Of course, I could always leave *you* up there, Snivelwurst."

"No! No! You wouldn't! Oh, ha, ha, what a wit

you are, your grace! Leave me — dear, dear, what a joke!"

"Well, if we don't find her," said Count Karlstein, "we'll have to leave someone else up there."

"May I suggest — " (sneeze) — "a certain young girl from the village here? The one I have in mind, sir, is she — " (sneeze) — "whom you lately employed as maid, Hildi Kelmar by name, sir."

"Interfering wench. I dismissed her this afternoon. Where is she now?"

"In the Jolly Huntsman, your grace. If I am not mistaken, it was she who gave the alarm of fire in the parlor a little while back, to our great discomfiture, your grace." (Sneeze.)

"A mischief-maker, eh? No one'll miss her, then. Not a bad idea, Snivelwurst...."

Now, that little conversation might have meant nothing at all to a lot of people. It would even have meant nothing to the great Cadaverezzi, I have no doubt. But it meant a good deal to *me,* because I was brought up by the most fearful, superstitious old band of ninnies there ever was. I was an orphan, you see, and in the orphanage in Geneva there was an old woman called Maria Neumann, who was in charge of all of us young blisters that was there, and she couldn't control us at all — poor old thing. We used to run riot. The only way she could make us do what we were told was by threatening us with the Demon Huntsman — the great and horrible Zamiel, the Prince of the Mountains, on his black horse, with his pack of luminous hounds and skeletons for his whippers-in. We shut up then all right. She used to smack her old lips together at the thought of us young ruffians being haunted by those frightful hounds — made our blood run cold. Even now it makes me shiver a bit; but then — under that bush, with two villains scheming some kind of devilry — to hear the name *Zamiel* gave me a proper turn.

Then the oily fellow sneezed sadly, and the count himself came out of the alley and set off down the road. He came within a foot of me, and I had a good look at him: a lean, wolfish, twitchy sort of individual, with a gnawing look about him — he might have been chewing the handle of his stick, now I come to think of it — and eyes with the white showing all round the pupil. Like his heart was being squeezed dry, making his eyes pop out. Disagreeable. I watched him stride off down the road, and then I got out of the bush and followed the oily-looking fellow. I hoped he'd go near the river, and he did — and I popped up by the bridge and beckoned to him.

"Shhh!" I said, putting my finger to my lips.

He crept up on tiptoe, like a stork in slippers. "What is it?" he said.

"Down there!" I whispered. "Shhh!"

"What?" He peered over the bridge.

"Down there in the shadows," I whispered.

"What? What?"

"Someone moving — look — lean over a bit more — "

"I can't see...."

So he leaned further out, and I tipped him in. Served him right. I let him yell and splash for a bit, and I yelled and roared as well to make him think he was drowning and being swept away, and then I went down the bank and hauled him out. He'd had a good soaking and he was starting to bubble a bit; and I laid him on a good sharp rock and knelt on him, to squeeze the water out, as I told him, and he yelled a good bit more, until windows opened and sleepy heads looked out and told us what they thought of it all. They knew some choice language, too.

"Did you see 'em?" I said.

"S-s-see who?" (Sneeze, sneeze, sneeze.)

"An Italian-looking feller and a little girl," I said, "creeping along the bank. They looked like they was up to no good."

"W-w-where did they go?" (Sneeze, sneeze.) "I m-m-must find them! E-m-m-mergency!" (Sneeze.)

I pointed — anywhere — and he was off, dripping and sneezing and squelching and shivering. Pathetic, of course; but I couldn't help being a little afraid of whatever it was that could make a spindly little runt like him so neglectful of his own comfort as to run about on a winter's night, still doing his master's business, even after a soaking like that. It must have been pretty powerful; so instead of laughing at him, I felt — as I said — afraid.

Oh, yes, Max Grindoff's not ashamed to admit it. I can be frightened sometimes. And I was more frightened than this before we'd finished.

However, I thought of what they'd said, those two, back in the alley—about the girl from the inn, Hildi, about how they'd give her to the Demon Huntsman instead of the Princess, if they couldn't find her. So I thought: the Jolly Huntsman's the next place for you, me boy — and about time too. A drop of brandy just now'd go down a treat.

That'll do for the time being. I've got to hand over to someone else now, so the young person can put down her pen and have a rest.

HILDI'S NARRATIVE
continued

I had to face Ma first, of course. She wasn't angry, which would have been bad enough, but hurt and sad, which was worse.

"Whatever did you do that for?" she said. "I was so looking forward to that little show, and you go and spoil it. I can't understand you, Hildi. You're as bad as Peter sometimes. I don't know...."

And she sat down heavily by the kitchen table and mopped her eyes with her apron. She looked old suddenly, and tired, and overcome. There was nothing I could say to comfort her; and there was plenty of clearing up to be done. Old Conrad, the barman, was still in the bar, because one or two of the men who'd been in earlier were still up, swapping stories and boasts about their shooting, and there was a great litter of mugs and glasses and dirty plates that everyone else seemed to have forgotten. I felt exhausted, and worried, and friendless and hopeless and everything-else-less.

Then, just as I was setting off for the kitchen with an armful of plates and a handful of mugs, the door opened and in came Doctor Cadaverezzi's servant, the one called Max. I looked at him in surprise, but what was more surprising was that he looked as if he expected to see me.

"Can I have a word, in private, like?" he said. Quietly, so the last fuddled drinkers in the bar shouldn't hear.

"Come in the kitchen," I said.

Ma had gone to bed. I put the plates and mugs down on the table and looked up to see him peering out of the back door.

"What are you doing?" I said. "There's no one out there!"

"Can't be too sure," he said. "Are you going to wash the dishes?"

"If there's any hot water," I said.

"I'll give you a hand. Let's get all them plates out here and then we can talk, in private, like what I said. It's important, else I wouldn't ask."

So we did. And when I'd looked in the copper to see if there was any hot water, and he'd ladled it out for me and refilled the copper from the well while I started to wash, he found a cloth and stood beside me in the candle-lit scullery and told me everything he knew. He worked well, too—quick and efficient and tidy. I liked him more and more. He stacked the plates properly and gave the knives and forks a good rub.

I listened without interrupting, and then I told him all I knew, and he listened without interrupting me. When I heard that Count Karlstein was planning to give *me* to Zamiel if he couldn't find Lucy, I shivered with fear; but when I heard that he'd treated Snivelwurst just as I'd done, I laughed out loud.

"But what it all boils down to," he said, when we'd finished and sat down by the fire, "is that we know where Miss Davenport is, and we think we know where Miss Charlotte is, but we don't know where Miss Lucy is, or where Doctor Cadaverezzi is; and Miss Davenport doesn't know where Miss Lucy is, and Doctor Cadaverezzi doesn't know where I am, and neither of the girls knows that Miss Davenport's here at all, or that Count Karlstein's still prowling about somewhere in the village, and—"

"I've lost track," I said. "We've got to find out if Charlotte's escaped—that's the main thing."

"But why?" he said. "I thought you put the key in her soup. She must have got out by now."

"But then Frau Muller found me in her parlor with the tray in my hand—they might have guessed what I was doing, and found the key! Or she might have been caught on the way out!"

"Hmm. Well, anyway, I reckon we ought to find Lucy first. I reckon that's the most important thing. Because—"

"No, because at least she's still free, so Count Karlstein hasn't got her, has he? But Charlotte may be still in the tower. So we might have to get her out—"

"We'll have to find Doctor Cadavarezzi—"

"We'll have to keep clear of the count—"

"We'll have to get into the castle—"

"We'll have to look in the mountain guide's hut—"

"We'll have to see Miss Davenport," we both said together. And we looked at each other across the old kitchen table, with the little candle burning low and the last ashes of the fire settling in the hearth, and reached out our hands and shook them solemnly.

"Now?" he said.

"Now," I said.

I got my cloak and wrapped it around myself, and we left. The village was asleep by now; the only light came from the parlor window of the inn, and as I looked back even that wavered and died away. Old Conrad was closing the bar.

The walk up to the woodcutter's hut took the best part of an hour. Max talked cheerfully at first, but even he couldn't keep it up for long; and tiredness, and apprehension, too, soon got the better of me. In the end we trudged along in silence, with only the crunch of our footsteps in the snow and the occasional cry of an owl breaking the vast quiet of the forest.

When we were nearly there, I stopped and looked around carefully. There was a path that led off to the left, but you wouldn't see it unless you knew where to look. I could see the flicker of a small fire as we shoved our way through the dense bushes and the snowy undergrowth, and then we were there.

But no one else was. The place was deserted.

"Where's she gone?" said Max.

"They can't have left very long ago or the fire would have gone out," I said. "These logs are fresh—look, they haven't been burning long."

Max took a burning stick out of the fire and, holding it like a torch, put his head inside the hut.

"No one in there," he said when he came out, "but all her things are there—that little cart of hers and her tent and so on—" He held the stick high and looked around.

And then, without any warning, a shot rang out from the trees, very close—so close I could see the flash of the powder at the same time as I heard the noise. And the stick Max was holding flew out of his hand and went spinning, like a firework, through the air behind him, and fell into the stream with a hiss. Then, in the ringing silence that followed, I heard very distinctly the sound of a little click. My brother, Peter, was a hunter; I'd heard guns since I was a baby, and I knew that sound well. It was the noise a hammer made, when it was raised to strike against the flint of a pistol. Whoever had fired the first shot was preparing to fire another; and he couldn't have wished for better targets than Max and me.

One day, I have no doubt, it will be as common for young ladies to be instructed in the arts of making a fire, of catching wild animals, and of skinning and cooking them, as it now is for them to be taught to paint in watercolors and to warble foolish ditties while attempting to accompany themselves upon the pianoforte. They do both of these things very badly, in my experience. In my Academy in Cheltenham I did try to instill some sense of adventure and enterprise into my girls, but, I am afraid, with little success. Who can prevail against Fashion? And these days it is the fashion for young girls to pretend to be frail, to languish, to swoon, to utter little fluting cries of rapture when they are pleased, and to lose consciousness altogether when they are not. Anything more ridiculous than the spectacle of

142

great stout red-faced girls of fifteen or sixteen attempting to be frail romantic heroines can scarcely be imagined. But they will do it; nothing will persuade them of how absurd they look; they will not be told otherwise, because it is the fashion. I wait, with such patience as I can muster, for the fashion, like the wind, to change and blow from another quarter. When that day comes, may Augusta Davenport be there still, to hail its dawning!

My maid Eliza is a case in point. Once her young man, Max Grindoff, had left us, I could see her become more nervous by the minute. It was quite instructive to watch—or it would have been, had I been able to see it. But darkness, of course, was necessary to the effect. Instead, I had to rely on her remarks.

—"Miss Davenport, do you believe in ghosts?"

—"Oh! Miss Davenport! I heard a spirit—I'm sure I did!"

—"Miss Davenport—did you see that horrid dark form hastening between the trees?"

—"Oh, Miss Davenport! What a frightful sound!"

(An owl, of course; but she would not believe it.)

—"Miss Davenport! A *bat*—I declare! Oh! Oh! Do you think it is a vampire?"

—"Oh, listen! Miss Davenport, can you hear the wolves? I'm sure it is wolves—"

By the time we reached our destination, the girl was nearly insensible with fear. Not real fear, of course—she is good-hearted enough to stand up bravely to real danger, if any had threatened—but imaginary fear; fashionable fear. No sense in scoffing at her, of course; so when we reached the woodcutter's hut, I set her to gathering some wood and lighting a fire while I explored a little way to see what I could discover about the lay of the land. Always a valuable exercise, this; once, in Turkestan, at the very edge of starvation, I surprised and shot a wild goat in just such circumstances. It was very tough, but it saved my life.

Nothing so nutritious showed itself this time, however, and I returned to the camp to find Eliza practically twittering with terror. I am afraid that I felt slightly impatient and I spoke sharply to her.

"Eliza, control yourself! Stop whimpering at me! Whatever is the matter with you?"

"Oh, Miss Davenport, I heard them, miss! There they were, the two of them, their poor little ghosts, drifting through the trees, miss!"

"What are you talking about?"

"The two little girls, miss!"

"Lucy and Charlotte? Are you sure?"

"They weren't alive, miss! They were spirits! Phantoms! Driven through the night, unable to rest anywhere, because of a curse that follows them to the ends of the earth! And, miss—"

"What *is* it, girl?"

"One of them was carrying her head in her arms, miss...."

"What?"

"She'd been beheaded—oh, it was terrifying, Miss Davenport—a little girl carrying her own head—her cloak was all pulled up high around her poor bare neck—I couldn't see no head on her shoulders at all, but there it was, in her arms—oh, I shall never forget it, not till my dying day...."

I thought for a moment that the girl had lost her reason. Ghosts carrying their own heads, indeed! But there had to be some kind of natural explanation. I questioned Eliza more closely.

From her answers it appeared that someone, whether or not the girls themselves, had gone past the woodcutter's hut only five minutes before; that there were two of them; and that they might easily have been the girls, if they were not so in fact. Obviously, we would have to follow them and find out. I took my pistols—both of them—and set out. Eliza, trembling, came with me.

But, of course, we found no trace of them. Snow in plenty; darkness in abundance; an excess of undergrowth; but no girls. Disappointed, but hardly surprised, I led the way back to our camp—only to hear voices there and to see a villainous-looking figure brandishing a flaming branch, intent (as I thought) upon setting fire to all our possessions. Which was foolish of me, I admit. I shot him; or, rather, shot the branch out of his hand, and then took my other pistol, ready to issue a stern warning.

And then Eliza took charge.

"Maxie!" she cried, and threw herself forward at the intruders.

"Eliza!" came the joyful reply, in the voice of the man Grindoff, and in a moment they were embracing.

"It's all right, Miss Davenport!" called Eliza, breathlessly. "It's Max!"

"So I see," I answered. "Grindoff, my man, I apologize for shooting at you. It was foolish of me. You are not hurt, are you?"

"Startled, ma'am, but not hurt," he said, as I stepped into the camp.

There was another person standing there—a girl of about fourteen, in a thin cloak. I had seen her before, in Castle Karlstein; I looked at her with great curiosity. Grindoff introduced her as Hildi Kelmar and told me all that had happened. The girl contributed, and it was clear from her first sentence that she was a much better witness than he was: clear where he was muddled, cool where he was indignant, intelligent where he was...well, less so.

"What do *you* think happened to the girls?" I said to her.

"What do *I* think, miss?" she said. "I think that Miss

Charlotte's got out, and I think she's gone down to the village looking for Miss Lucy, and I think they've found each other and gone back up to the mountain guide's hut, where I took 'em first. If only they'd stayed there, miss!"

"Quite, quite," I said. "I agree. Something of the sort must have happened. It is a shame, Grindoff, that you did not go up to the castle as I directed—"

"I wish I had, now, ma'am," he said. "But I honestly thought Doctor Cadaverezzi would make a better job of it, like."

"He sounds a remarkable man, indeed," I said, though I considered privately that if he had been *that* remarkable, he would not have exposed Lucy to the danger of being captured. "But he has disappeared, you say?"

"Vanished into thin air, ma'am," he said. "It's just like his illusion of the Disappearing Dervish. What happens is, this little Dervish—clockwork he is, and a proper marvel—anyway, the doctor sets him going, whirling about on a solid table, and then—"

"Yes, yes. Perhaps when Doctor Cadaverezzi rematerializes from the dimension into which he has temporarily retired, he will be so kind as to demonstrate the Disappearing Dervish to us. In the meantime, there seems to be no alternative but to follow the girls to the mountain guide's hut. Is it very far, Hildi?"

"A couple of hours' walk, miss," she said, looking at

me doubtfully. I understood that look perfectly: it said, You're old and fat and you won't make it. I took it as a challenge.

"Let us go, then," I said, rising to my feet. "If anyone is tired, then he or she need not come. One volunteer, after all, is worth ten pressed men." I spoke with perfect confidence. Each of them privately shared Hildi's opinion. Each of them, therefore, would have been ashamed to see me set off, and stay behind themselves. So, naturally, all three volunteered to come with me.

"Excellent," I said comfortably.

We arrived at the mountain guide's hut just as the moon was setting. Dawn, clearly, was not far off, and little Hildi was leaning on my arm (though she did not realize it). It was a wild, deserted spot, on the very edge of the heights; an awesome prospect revealed itself to us: a mighty glacier, vast banks of pure snow, jagged cliffs, and tumbled rocks. It was all silvered by the dying moonlight, and an intense cold struck through us like a spear; not only a physical cold, either, but the cold of fear. How could anyone survive in this wilderness? I prayed that the girls would have had the sense to stay in the hut this time—always supposing that they had not perished on the way and we had missed their frozen bodies.

So it was with considerable trepidation that I opened

the door; and our disappointment, on seeing the place empty, was almost too much to be borne. Still, I determined that we should not despair. I told Grindoff and Eliza to search the hut; there would probably be nothing there, but it would keep them occupied. Meanwhile, I took my telescope and went outside to look for any traces of the girls.

I saw their footprints in the snow—but that was hardly surprising, since I knew they had been there. I saw another set of footprints, which I took to be Hildi's—and called her out, to check. They were. And it was she who pointed out to me that there were more prints—the girls'—all around the hut.

"It must have been after I left here, miss," she said. "They must have come out to look around. They haven't half trodden it about!"

It was true: the snow for some distance around the hut was disturbed. To my relief, there seemed to be no other prints but theirs. Hildi had moved a little further up the mountainside, and I saw her suddenly dart forward and peer closely at the ground. Then she turned and beckoned.

"What is it?" I said as I arrived at her side—but she had no need to answer, for there, clearly printed in the snow, were two sets of prints.

"They're gone!" she said.

"Up the mountain, too. Oh, how vexing. How very vexing."

"They can't have been gone long, miss," she said.

Just then Eliza came hurrying out of the hut, waving a piece of paper.

"Look! Look, Miss Davenport! Look what we've found!"

It was a note, in a handwriting which I recognized as Lucy's. I had tried, during the time in which she was in my care, to persuade her to form her letters with some degree of elegance, but in vain; she suffers, as do so many others, from the delusion that neat handwriting is dull while scrawled handwriting is interesting and attractive. I cannot understand this idea. Fashion, again. I consoled myself with the reflection that at least I had taught her to punctuate. The note read:

TO WHOM IT MAY CONCERN:

    Tormented by Fate, cheated of Hope, and exiled by the Cruelty of one from whom we should have expected Kindness and Friendship, we have resolved to offer ourselves up to the Powers of the eternal snows, in the sure knowledge that there can be no less Mercy among the crags and glaciers than among the tapestries and paneled walls of our late dwelling place, CASTLE KARLSTEIN.

                    Farewell forever.

I read this aloud to the others as we sat round the fire and then laid it down—with, I confess, great weariness.

"What are they playing at?" said Grindoff. "I don't understand it, miss. What are they running away for?"

"I told you, Max!" said Hildi. "Zamiel!"

He shook his head. "I'm fair wore out," he said. "It slipped me mind altogether. Fancy forgetting that...."

"Zamiel?" I inquired. "Enlighten me, pray."

So Hildi did. She recounted all that she had heard; and then Grindoff repeated what he had heard Count Karlstein say to his secretary, that watery individual, in the alley beside the Mayor's house.

"I see," I said. And then I sat back and closed my eyes, the better to think.

Many parts of central Europe—some parts of Britain—have their legends about the Wild Hunt. Windsor Park, so it is said, is haunted by Herne the Hunter; it is an ancient and very interesting superstition. Superstition? Does that mean I did not believe in it? Oh, no. A closed mind is a dead mind. If I did not believe in it, Count Karlstein certainly did, and was going to base a particularly malevolent action on this belief. I saw no reason to assume that any of this was nonsense, and several reasons to assume that it was true. But for every malevolent force there were remedies—charms, protections, call them what you will. I tried to recall what I had read.

But the question that presented itself constantly was, of course, what was to be done? A bargain had been struck, it seemed. Count Karlstein had agreed, in return for some favor that he had either received already or would receive in the future, to provide a victim or victims for Zamiel the Demon Hunter. They were to be delivered to him at midnight on All Souls' Eve—which, as I saw by first opening my eyes and then consulting my *Gentlewoman's Tropical Almanac*, was the very day that was now dawning. I closed my eyes again and recommenced my survey of the problem.

The Demon Huntsman was going to appear in the hunting lodge at midnight, there to receive his tribute. It was clear that no particular victim was specified, for Count Karlstein had been heard to say that if Lucy and Charlotte were not available, Hildi would do instead. What would happen if there were no one there at all when midnight struck? Clearly, Count Karlstein would be held by the demon to have failed in his duty. Hence the man's insane anxiety.

And would not the wrath of the demon then recoil upon Count Karlstein himself? That was less clear. It might be that any human beings in the forest nearby— peasants, woodcutters, and the like—would be in danger; and that the demon, having satisfied his hunger, would leave Count Karlstein alone. Without more information on the habits of demons, I was unable to say for certain.

I then turned my attention to Count Karlstein himself, and what I knew of his relation to the girls. He was a cousin of their unfortunate mother's. She had died, together with their father, Sir Percival, in a shipwreck; it had been my melancholy duty to inform the girls of their loss and to make the arrangements for their journey to Switzerland. Count Karlstein was their only living relative. He had at first, I recalled, been reluctant to receive them into his home, but the persuasion of the family lawyer—a most excellent gentleman called Haifisch—had changed his mind; and I had seen them off on the first stage of their journey with some anxiety.

Something was stirring in my memory, as I knew it would if I leaned back and closed my eyes.

Haifisch—Karlstein—the girls...I should have to go to Geneva.

I sat up, opened my eyes, and clapped my hands to awaken the others. Hildi's red-rimmed eyes turned toward me, and the ghost of a snore was suddenly cut off by its perpetrator, Grindoff, who sat up briskly and yawned so wide that I fancied for a moment that I heard his jaws creak.

"What is it, Miss Davenport?" said Eliza sleepily.

I explained, in detail. They agreed: there was nothing else for it. So we set off, in our different directions—and in as much haste as we could manage to summon. The affair was more serious now. Previously, it had been a matter of two lost children; now it was a matter of life and death. There was no time to lose.

Lucy's Narrative
continued

I suppose that if you fell from a mighty cliff and had the good fortune to land on a ledge a little way down, shaken but unhurt, you would feel your Despair give way to relief; and I suppose that if that ledge were to crumble beneath you and precipitate you further into the abyss, your first Despair might well be redoubled; and if that were to happen yet again, you might well wonder whether some evil power were taking a personal interest in your affairs. Thus I felt, when I ran out of the police station after Doctor Cadaverezzi's arrest.

Fleeing from Castle Karlstein, we had foolishly left the mountain hut and lost each other. Charlotte had been captured straight away, by that maggot in human form, Arturo Snivelwurst; but I had found Doctor Cadaverezzi, and safety. (And I had enjoyed being a

Princess, too. I think it is a role that I might be good in: that of actress, I mean, or strolling player, or mounte-bankess.) Then came the danger again—Count Karlstein spotted me in the tavern. Then came safety—Hildi, rais-ing the false alarm of fire, enabled us to get away. Then, yet again, danger—and poor Doctor Cadaverezzi was arrested. (Although, if I knew him, he would not stay arrested for long. I had known him only a short time— merely a matter of hours—but in that time he had impressed me with the force of his Genius in a way that no one, not even Miss Davenport, had done before. I felt as if his mind inhabited a larger, freer, more glorious Universe than this one, and though I tried to reproach him for his misdeeds, I knew that they were nothing beside the glory of his Imagination and the unbounded radiance of his spirit. Ah, well. I had heard—as Charlotte, for instance, had not—the most intoxicating of all sounds: the applause of the public....)

But we were cruelly disappointed now. It was not difficult for us to decide what we should do; we reached the mountain guide's hut in less than an hour, but there was no point in staying there, since Hildi, we knew, would be captured by the count and tortured to reveal all she knew. She would hold out as long as she could, but eventually the rack and the thumbscrews would overcome her and, fainting, in the last extremity of Anguish she would gasp out that this had been our hiding place. Then the count would hasten, snarling, to the kennels, unleash the ferocious hounds, and...

So there was nothing for it but to climb the mountains. Italy, after all, lay on the other side.

We were lucky that it was not snowing. The brilliant moonlight showed us every crag, every rocky cliff, every precipice, every glinting carapace of ice. I do not know what a carapace is, but I am sure there were some on the mountain. At first the exhilaration of climbing, even in our weariness, kept us going. The unearthly beauty of the scene—like some Vision from the works of Byron or Shelley—filled our hearts with strange longings. It was easy to believe, in that dreamlike setting, in the Spirits and Phantoms of folklore. We climbed and climbed, until all feeling had been lost from our feet and hands, and until every breath was a sharp pain in our lungs, but we dared not stop. We climbed until the moon set behind the glittering jagged edge of the mountainside, and then we went on climbing in the horrid chill that fell with the darkness—a deeper chill than ever before. But the sky was lightening. Some of the stars in the region to our left were beginning to fade, as the light soaked up the dark blue they rested on—they faded as pearls are supposed to fade if they are not worn. (Although I have never possessed any pearls, my dear mother had a fine necklace of them, which was with her when the ship sank; so that they returned to their element as she left hers, forever! I think there is something malign about jewelry, and I will not wear it for that reason. No! Not even the simplest gold ring. I have made a Vow.)

And presently, with a grandeur that none who have not seen it can possibly imagine, the sun rose over the Alps.

We were, at that point, on a kind of small plateau in the ice. To our right, a great sheet of snow sparkled and gleamed, leading up to a vast cliff of dark rock. Ahead of us, in tumbled profusion, jagged lumps of ice, some as small as Charlotte's Herr Woodenkopf and some as big as a cottage, lay scattered over the surface of the glacier. To our left, the sun, unbearably bright, rose like a stately balloon with a cargo of the original fire of the gods, over a ridge of sharp-edged snow. There were no shadows in this icy world, because instead of hiding the light or keeping it out, the ice magnified it and split it up in the way Sir Isaac Newton did in his famous experiment, which Miss Davenport demonstrated to us one bright morning in Cheltenham, by means of a prism. So, instead of shadows, there were rainbows everywhere.

Dazzled, we walked on. Charlotte clung to her bewigged head with one hand and to me with the other, and she stumbled along with her eyes shut, either because she was fast asleep or because the sunlight hurt them. I, too, found it difficult to see. There seemed to be little flickering movements just at the edge of my eyes, and I thought I was becoming Intoxicated or Delirious.

Then Charlotte spoke.

"Lucy, I cannot walk another step!" she said. "I'm going to faint."

"If we lie down here, we shall die," I told her. "We shall freeze in a moment and become like the mummy in Signor Rolipolio's Exhibition."

She shuddered and clutched Herr Woodenkopf even tighter to her chest.

"All wrinkled and horrid?" she said.

"Very wrinkled and extremely horrid. No, Charlotte, we must keep going."

"But we'll never find a way through *that—*" she said,

pointing at the glacier and squinting with the effort to see what she was pointing at. "We'll fall into a crevasse, like Otto, in *The Secrets of the North,* and get crushed flat. We'll get lost and go round in circles and go mad. Oh, Lucy, I just can't. We've come as far as this—they'll never find us now—please let's rest...."

I was exhausted too, of course, but as the elder I had to pretend not to be. Such is the Responsibility of age and experience. There are no corresponding rewards that I have discovered, but that is by the way.

"No!" I said. "We must move on. Think of the south, Charlotte!"

"I can't...."

"Of course you can if you try. Think of...orange trees and olive groves and things like that."

"I don't like olives."

"All right, think of melons then. Hot things."

"Melons are cold...."

"You're being very trying, Charlotte," I said sternly.

"I *am* trying," she said, having misheard me. So I said nothing more but merely tugged her onward. She fell three times, and bruised her legs, and began to cry, and Herr Woodenkopf's wig came off and had to be put back on, and her dress was soaked and mine was torn, and then I twisted my foot slipping on the ice, and then Charlotte fell for a fourth time and just lay there, still, crying, and I thought: no, no! This is the End. We shall die. We shall die. We shall die....

There was a sort of darkness in the air around us.

I felt colder and colder, and I longed to pull that hovering darkness down and wrap it around us like a blanket. I know now that the darkness was Death; but even knowing that, I would have pulled it down, if I could.

I heard a voice, and felt a hand upon my shoulder. Charlotte was shaking me.

"Lucy!" I heard her say. "Lucy! That's the man I saw in the forest—Lucy, wake up!"

There was a little stream, somehow unfrozen in the ice, that ran and splashed and threw up tiny fountains of spray that sparkled like flying diamonds. And beyond the stream stood a man, calling us. He had an honest face and very bright blue eyes. He waved when he saw that we'd woken, and crossed the stream by jumping carefully from one rock to another. He looked tired. When he stood in front of us, he said, "I don't need to ask who you are. There's only one pair of girls on this mountain, I reckon. Here, I've got a letter for you."

I thought I must be dreaming. But the paper he handed me—warm from an inside pocket—was real enough,
so real that I recognized it as the note I'd scribbled in
the mountain guide's hut.

"But I wrote this," I said, and my voice shook.

"Turn it over, miss," he said.

I did—and leapt up straight away when I recognized
the handwriting.

"Charlotte! Look! Miss Davenport!"

She sprang up too and leaned over to look at the
note, and together we read it quickly.

It said:

My dear Lucy and Charlotte,

   You may trust the bearer of this note with
your lives. Please come down with him
straight away. We shall discuss what is to be
done when we are together. Lucy, your handwriting
is atrocious. You must endeavor to correct it.

                              Your good friend,
                              Augusta Davenport

"Lucy, it's her! It really is!" cried Charlotte.

I was nearly as delighted—but not quite. I pride

myself upon my handwriting. I think it is distinguished, mature, and interesting.

"Well, shall we go, then?" said the man.

"Oh! Sorry—yes, of course!" I replied.

He was flapping his arms and stamping his feet, trying to look as if it was quite normal to be standing several thousands of feet up a snowy mountain.

"What is your name?" I said. "I'm Lucy, and this is Charlotte."

"Max Grindoff," he said, and we shook hands. He pointed to Herr Woodenkopf, beaming up at us from a boulder, his wig askew. "Good thing you set him up there," he said. "I'd never have seen you else. He caught me eye as I came along—I couldn't see you two at all, being as how you was lying down, like."

Charlotte was overjoyed, and hugged Herr Woodenkopf tight. "See!" she said triumphantly. "I knew he was lucky!"

"I been having a rare old traipse about on account of you," said Max. "Come along down and I'll tell you what's been going on. Are you the Princess, then?"

"Yes! But how do you know? Have you seen Doctor Cadaverezzi? Is he out of jail?"

"So that's where he is! I might have known. I'm his servant, see. Well, if he's in jail there's nothing to worry about—he'll be out in no time. Whenever it suits him, he'll tell some tale to the sergeant and stroll out of the front door as cool as you please. He's a wonder, that man."

And so, as we went down the mountain again, we heard from Max of everything that had happened. I found a strange feeling growing in my heart, one that had been uprooted and trampled down many times already, so that I thought it had died forever: I mean, Hope.

HILDI'S NARRATIVE
continued

Miss Davenport, with the aid of a pocket lens, had constructed a fire by the time the girls came down with Max; and although not even her gifts could conjure food out of thin air, so that we were all hungry, at least we had some warmth.

But the fire itself was no warmer than her greeting of them, and their joy at seeing her. I suppose if I'd been parted from Ma under conditions of extreme danger, I'd have fallen into her arms with the same kind of joy when I found her again; but I never had, thank God, and I could only imagine it. However, when she began to explain her plan, the chill entered their expressions once more, and I found my own blood freezing at the thought of it.

"The essential thing," she said, "is to make the

vengeance of Zamiel recoil upon Count Karlstein. That will happen only if the demon is cheated of his prey. However, if *you* are not available, the count will simply substitute someone else—and so not only sacrifice an innocent life, but escape himself."

"What can we do, Miss Davenport?" asked Lucy.

"You must go back to the castle and let him take you to the hunting lodge."

"What!" exclaimed Charlotte.

"Oh, yes. It is essential that the count believe that you are there, and that he is therefore safe. That way, you see, he will neglect to take precautions—and Zamiel will find no obstacle when he arrives at the castle."

"But—" I began.

She held up her hand. "I know what you are going to say, Hildi. Why should Zamiel turn upon Count Karlstein if he has victims ready at hand in the hunting lodge? And how are the girls going to survive? The answer to that is simple: you and your brother will go there and rescue them."

I was amazed.

"The principle," she explained, "is quite simple. There are a number of substances which are known to ward off demons and other supernatural beings. Garlic is one of them. Its effectiveness, in the case of the Transylvanian Vampire, is well known. Another such substance is silver."

I began to understand. Max was scratching his head, and Eliza, whose red-rimmed eyes showed how tired she was, was gazing at Miss Davenport and trying to follow that learned lady's explanation.

"And we've got garlic in our kitchen," I said.

"Plenty, I hope. And then there is the silver. Has anyone any silver jewelry?"

"I wear no jewelry," said Lucy. "It is a matter of Principle."

Charlotte shook her head helplessly, but Eliza took a little chain from around her neck.

"I've got this, miss," she said, "only it's very precious, because Maxie gave it to me, if you please, miss." It was the broken half of a small silver coin. Miss Davenport examined it closely.

"How very curious," she said. "But it is too small for our purpose, I fear. Well—there is nothing for it. We shall have to use *this*." So saying, she took a large and very handsome silver bracelet from her wrist. It was a lovely thing: like a solid chain, with a rim on either side set with delicate beads, like dew, and deep and lustrous in color.

"That was a present from…one who was very dear to me," she said.

"Signor Rolipolio!" said Eliza. "Sorry, miss."

"That will do, Eliza. But you are quite right. However, its chemical composition is what matters, not its tender associations. Your brother, Hildi," she went on, turning to me, "will have to cast this into the form of a bullet."

"Peter, miss? But—"

"I am sure he will be able to manage it. Every huntsman can cast bullets. The melting point of silver, though, is considerably higher than that of lead; it may take some time. It would be as well to start soon."

There was no standing up to her. I was to go with Peter, it seemed, him with a silver bullet in his gun and me with pocketfuls of garlic, and rescue the girls from the hunting lodge. The silver bullet was a last resort, since the idea was not to destroy Zamiel (some hope, I thought privately) so much as to baffle him and turn him back on the count. We'd need horses, too, to bring the girls back to safety afterward.

"And what'll you do, miss?" said Eliza.

"This matter will not be finished until certain inquiries have been made. I shall have to make them personally; so I must leave for Geneva at once. You, Eliza, and Grindoff must take the girls to the castle—make sure you deliver them into the hands of the count himself and tell him some story about finding them lost in the woods. Girls, you must appear full of remorse, but without any suspicion at all. As for you, Hildi, your part is very dangerous, I do not deny it; but I have every confidence in you. And now we must leave this very comfortable hut and make our separate ways down the mountain...."

As I made my way down (stumbling with weariness and clutching the bracelet tight so as not to lose it), the only thing I could think was: where's Peter going to forge the bullet?

But as it turned out, that was the easiest part of the whole business. He listened to me in silence, sleepy-eyed and still and unshaven, and took the bracelet without a word and went up to the kitchen.

"Peter! What about Ma? And Sergeant Snitsch, and everything?"

"Keep 'em out of the way," was all he said, and he began to pile the fire high. It was still early; only Hannerl the serving girl and old Conrad the barman were up and about. And before Ma came down, I was falling asleep. I had a confused impression of someone smelling of soot and smoke laying me down on a bed and covering me with an eiderdown, and then I slept properly.

I awoke in the late afternoon, with a cold gray light sifting in through the window. My head was all stuffy and headachy, and something was making me anxious, but I didn't know what it was....And then I remembered and ran downstairs.

The kitchen was as hot as the blacksmith's forge. The windows were streaming, the air was full of smoke, there was a pile of ashes ankle deep in front of the hearth; and there at the table, his face streaked with soot and red-eyed with smoke, sat Peter. In front of him was a little ball of clay, as big as a duck's egg. He was feeling it carefully with the palm of his hand.

"What's happening?" I said. "Where's Ma?"

"In the parlor."

"What about the bullet? Is it ready?"

"I'm just about to find out." He took a knife and, holding it by the blade, tapped the clay mold once or twice with the handle. Nothing happened. He paused, and looked at me directly. "You realize what this means, if I come with you tonight?" he said.

I nodded. "The contest," I said.

"That's right. I've got to win it, Hildi. It's my last chance. I can't afford to lose now."

He was right. I knew what he'd be risking, and I knew as well as he did that the night ahead of us would be the very worst sort of preparation for the contest in the morning. There was nothing I could say. He tapped the mold again, harder, and it cracked and fell apart. The two halves rocked back and forth on the tabletop. Embedded in one of them, like the stone in a peach, lay a perfect silver ball.

"You beauty!" he cried. He picked it up tenderly and tapped the rest of the mold so that the ball came free, on a long stalk of silver where the molten metal had run down the channel he'd left for it in the clay. "Taken me all day, this," he said. "I lost half of it, and all, when the first mold broke. What a beauty, eh!" He began to file off the stalk, while I filled my pockets with bulbs of garlic.

"What about horses?" I said.

"Hannerl's seeing to them."

"I wish we didn't need them...."

"Well, we do. It's a long way—we'll have to bring the girls back as well, don't forget. And we don't want to leave it too late." He looked up at the old wooden clock—half-past four, it said.

If we left now, we'd do it easily. After five o'clock, and we'd be pushing it a bit—any later than that, and we'd probably not make it before midnight; in which case we might as well give up now....But I still wished we didn't need horses. I don't like horses, or they don't like me; and though I could manage old Pansy, that was because she could manage only a walk.

Peter held up the bullet again to admire it and looked up briefly as the door opened and Hannerl came in from the stables. She was a soft, kindly girl of sixteen, much in love with Peter, who was (I supposed) handsome in a scowling sort of way.

"I've found a pair," she said. "I've saddled 'em up for you."

"Whose are they?" said Peter.

It was seldom that we had more than two or three horses in the stable, but now that the inn was full there were a dozen or more.

"I don't know who they belong to exactly, but they won't want 'em tonight and that's a fact. They're all settled in the parlor with their pipes."

"Good girl," he said, and the silly thing blushed.

I went into the parlor to say good-bye to Ma, feeling horribly uneasy about a number of things—of which riding a horse was by no means the least. Ma came to one side with me while old Conrad knocked out the bung of a barrel of beer. I didn't know what Peter had told her; I'd have to go carefully.

"Well?" she said.

"We've got to go out. To the forest. Honestly, Ma, we've got to."

"All right, I won't ask any more. That boy's said nothing to me all day—I can't get any sense out of him. For God's sake, Hildi—I don't know what's going on, but look after him, will you?"

"Me—look after him?"

"Don't let him shoot at the police, that's all I ask. It'll be his life then, not a few weeks in jail. And that'd be the end of me. I couldn't bear it, Hildi." And she started to cry, suddenly and very quietly. I tried to comfort her, but she wiped her eyes and pushed me away. "That's all I ask," she said thickly. "Go on now, get away."

She pushed me again, and I left her, my heart full of all kinds of unhappiness. She'd caused a picture of Peter to come into my mind: bare-headed, shirt-sleeved, in chains, with a guard on either side and a black-robed chaplain, and the chilly gray light of dawn illuminating the brutal timbers and the hateful blade of a guillotine. I thrust the picture away as quickly as I could and hurried back into the kitchen.

"Come on," he said. "What's the matter?"

"You're not to shoot any policemen."

"Oh, is that it? Come on, let's get out—"

But we got no further than the kitchen door. All of a sudden Hannerl ran in, her face white, and pushed the door shut behind her.

"What is it?" said Peter.

"He's out there—the sergeant—in the stable—" said Hannerl, in a desperate whisper. "He came in just now with someone to look at a horse—I had to take the saddles off them other two and pretend I was putting 'em away. You'll have to hide! He might come in here!"

Peter's face darkened. He glanced at the clock again: a quarter to five. How long would the sergeant be?

"Get in the cellar," I whispered. "Go on. I'll get rid of him somehow. But get out of sight, for goodness' sake."

He went unwillingly and I turned to go through to the stable—only to find the sergeant himself entering the kitchen, and taking off his helmet, and mopping his brow, and sitting down at the table...."Phew!" he said.

173

"What's been going on in here? Trying to burn the place down?"

"What do you want?" I said.

"I want to sit down and have a glass of beer, that's what I want. I'd like a word with your ma. Where is she?"

"What do you want to talk to her about?"

For answer he tapped his great red nose and said nothing. Hannerl was hovering uncertainly in the doorway to the stable; and Peter, I knew, would be crouched at the top of the cellar steps, listening to every word.

And then Ma came in and saw the sergeant and stamped in vexation.

"Oh! It's too bad!" she said. "I've got an inn full of guests, people coming and going all day long, no help to speak of—and you come and park yourself right in the middle of it. What do you want?"

"Now, now, Frau Kelmar," he said soothingly. "The fact is, I thought I'd pop round for a chat."

"I haven't got time," she snapped. "Out—go on! Be off with you! You're only in the way here."

She slammed down some saucepans on the table beside his elbow and shook some flour into a bowl, taking care that some of it fell on his uniform. I went through to the stables with Hannerl, shutting the door behind me, and said:

"Come on—let's get those horses saddled again. As soon as she gets rid of him, we can leave."

"No!" she said. "He's talking about buying a horse—they'll be in and out, I shouldn't wonder!"

"Oh, no! How long's it going to take, for goodness' sake?"

She shook her head as the clock in the church tower struck five. I sat down on the step. The sergeant's voice droned on behind the door, interrupted by the clatter of saucepans and the occasional tart remark from Ma. Time passed.

I said to Hannerl, "It's no good—we'll have to saddle them up and take the risk. Maybe we can take them outside and wait in the alley."

"But supposing—"

"We'll just have to hope they don't. Where are the horses you picked out?"

She showed me a great black brute and a skittish-looking bay. I didn't like the look of either of them, but I helped her get them ready, and then went back to the door. The sergeant was still there, and another man's voice joined in as well now: old Conrad was saying something.

The clock struck half-past five.

"Oh, won't he *ever* go?" I whispered. "Hannerl, go and tell him there's been a burglary somewhere and they want him quick—"

But then came the sound of a chair being pushed back, and the sergeant laughing.

"He's going," whispered Hannerl. "He might come back out this way...."

We waited; more time passed. I was near to despair. Finally I could stand it no longer and opened the door and entered the kitchen. Ma was busy at the fire, her expression tight and furious. The sergeant was standing in the doorway to the parlor, talking to someone.

"Ma! Go through and shut the door and I'll get Peter out quickly!" I whispered.

She nodded, and pushed past the sergeant, shutting the door. I opened the cellar door, and Peter, sitting on the top step, leapt up in a moment. "Where is he?" he said.

"Come on! Let's go!" I whispered. I looked at the clock before I shut the door: a quarter to six....

Peter, snarling and cursing with frustration, swung himself up onto the black horse, and Hannerl struggled to keep the bay still while I mounted. Peter's horse snorted with impatience while I said, "Good horse—nice old thing—be gentle, now—" and similar daft things. The horse tossed his head scornfully, Hannerl opened the door, and we were off.

It was dark. There were lights in the windows of the houses we rode past; a little snow was falling, just swirling fretfully about, trying to make up its mind whether to land or fly on for a bit. Peter rode straight off at a trot, not looking to right or left. My horse wasn't keen on the snow, and I didn't blame him, but I wished he wouldn't skip about.

I managed to stay on until we came to the bridge.

This was going to be the most dangerous part. The bridge was always busy; it was the only place for miles where you could cross the river, and the road wasn't an unimportant one: there were always travelers coming and going, besides the villagers themselves and us up at the castle. So I wasn't surprised to see two or three men strolling across from the other side. They were strangers; they looked as if they'd been for a walk, for they weren't carrying any luggage, nor were they dressed for a long journey. One of them was holding a lantern. They stood aside to let us by; and then suddenly one of them gaped and gripped the arm of the man with the lantern.

"That's my horse!" he cried, pointing at the black that Peter was riding.

Peter cursed and drove his heels into the horse's sides to kick it on. The man leapt into the road in front of him.

"Ringl! Ringl!" he cried, waving his arms, and tried to seize the reins as Peter, galloping now, swept past. But the man missed his footing, slipped on the icy road, and fell heavily—right under the hooves of my horse! I screamed, and Peter yelled something up ahead and the other two men shouted, too; and my horse leapt and seemed to spring sideways and missed the man who'd fallen. But I was nearly out of the saddle and I'd lost a stirrup and one hand was clutching the horse's mane while the other tugged fearfully at the reins; and as I twisted, trying to find the stirrup and my balance simultaneously, one of the other men jumped forward and seized the reins—and the horse's head slewed round suddenly, and I fell.

It didn't hurt at first. I was too shocked. I scrambled to my feet and ran, while the men shouted at me to stop and the horse neighed and whinnied with excitement and fear, and other shouts from behind told me that the rest of the village had heard. How long before the police arrived? I felt sick with disappointment.

Peter had vanished. I hoped he'd managed to see what had happened, so he wouldn't wait for me; we'd lost too much time as it was. There'd be an alarm out for sure; the horses would be traced back to the Jolly Huntsman, Ma would be questioned, and—

I sank into the snow under the shelter of the trees and the gathering darkness. I felt like weeping. Before it had even begun, our plan was in ruins. Behind me on the bridge, the little knot of men pointed after Peter, held the plunging horse, helped up the man who'd fallen, shouted for help, and began to stream over the bridge in pursuit. The sergeant was leading them; they were armed with muskets....

I lay still, the cold seeping through my dress and straight into my heart, and my pockets full of the now useless garlic. It was all up to Peter now—and a little ball of silver. But would he be in time?

Lucy's Narrative
continued

Triumph is a grim quality! Especially when it is not yours but another's. And especially when that other is a knuckle-chewing, twitching, icy-eyed uncle with a smile like the snarl of a tiger. He welcomed us—that is to say, Charlotte and me and Max and Eliza—into his study with an air of such slinking, smirking, purring greed that I nearly turned tail and ran away at once.

We'd decided to say nothing. Max spoke, and Uncle Heinrich rubbed his hands together and never for one moment let his eyes stray from the two of us. I tried to outstare him, but the chilly gleam was too much for me and I had to look down.

"We found 'em up the mountain, sir," Max was saying. "They was wandering about lost. It seemed the kindest thing to bring 'em home, like."

"Very good—very good...." said Uncle Heinrich. "Very pleased to see them....Dear little things! My poor little poppets! They've come home to Uncle Heinrich...." And so on, while his eyes flickered icily up and down from our heads to our toes, and his hands, white-knuckled, rubbed each other with a never-ceasing little *shush-shush* noise, and his lips grinned stiffly.

"They've been ever so frightened, your grace," said Eliza. "Someone's been putting wicked tales into their heads. They didn't know what they were doing, I swear they didn't."

"Yes—yes—I'm sure you're right. Poor little things! So cold and hungry! Are you hungry, girls? Mmm? Answer me, now. Are you hungry?"

"Yes, Uncle Heinrich," I said. I had to speak; he was gripping my cheek between his finger and thumb in a gesture which I suppose might have looked tender from a distance.

He released my cheek, and I rubbed it while he rang the bell. Then he turned to Max and Eliza again and fumbled in the drawer of his desk.

"Here," he said, and gave them some money. "Take this, with my thanks."

"Thank you, sir," said Max, and tugged his forelock. I could see he didn't enjoy it; he was a bad actor at the best of times and I wondered how he'd ever managed to perform beside Doctor Cadaverezzi. But Uncle Heinrich was in too triumphant a mood to notice things like that, and he patted Max on the back and then (horror!) came between Charlotte and me, put an arm around us both and hugged us. We stood very still.

Then Frau Muller, that sour personage, came in to take us away to be fed—and, I knew, locked up until required, like luggage on board ship. We didn't say good-bye to Max and Eliza—there didn't seem to be time—but Eliza gave us a swift smile when Uncle Heinrich had turned to speak to Frau Muller, and Max winked. But they looked as anxious as we felt, and I thought (for the ninetieth time): Have we done the right thing?

Once we were out of sight of our supposed rescuers, there was no doubt that we were prisoners. Frau Muller spoke to us harshly, and Wilhelm the groom—an uncouth individual and a brute with the horses—stood guard over us while we ate, in Frau Muller's austere parlor, some thin gruel and dry bread. She allowed us a cup of wine each, which, being thirsty, we drank at once; and hardly had the last mouthful of food vanished down our throats than we both yawned and nodded with exhaustion. I remember thinking: This is odd, they're watching us, and there's someone else arrived—oh, it's Herr Snivelwurst—he's sneezed all over Charlotte, but she hasn't noticed—she's fast asleep—someone's lifted me up—I'm falling asleep too....

And then, nothing but a rushing darkness, filled with strange impressions that loomed like dreams and then sank out of sight: cold; and jolting discomfort; the sound of horses; something that creaked like dry leather; a face thrust close to mine, with an air of stale brandy about it; something that scratched my cheek, like a rough blanket; and finally, silence, and sleep again—the deepest sleep I'd ever known.

Hours went by. I think that what woke me in the end was the ticking. Some clocks are distinctive, with personalities—friendly or malicious as the case may be. I see no reason to deny personality to a machine, in this age of marvels, when natural philosophy is daily plumbing the Mysteries of Life itself. I recognized this clock, and I did not like it. It had a malevolent wheeze. An ancient, fragile creaking from deep inside the case told of how it was gathering its strength for the next *tick*— and they were very slow and somber, these ticks, as if each one might be its last—or yours....

It was the clock in the hunting lodge. We were there, captive!

I was awake in an instant. I found I was lying on a rug in front of the hearth and that I had been wrapped tightly in several blankets; too tightly to move. Or was I bound? I struggled, with panic rising in my breast, but found that there were no ropes, at least. There was no fire in the hearth and it was bitterly cold. I sat up. Charlotte lay beside me, similarly wrapped. I shook her, and the movement made me feel very sick and sent blows of pain resounding through my head. She would not wake, and I had not the strength to shake her again. I lay back trembling.

The darkness was not quite total. There was one small window, which looked out at the close-packed ranks of dark trees, and through this a fragment of moonlight, inexpressibly melancholy, filtered hazily. As the throbbing in my head subsided, I looked around and saw by this dim and gloomy radiance that we were alone. Ugly lumps of black shadows thrust themselves out from the rough wooden walls like gargoyles:

hunting trophies, the heads of bears and stags slaughtered by the count or his predecessors. It was my fancy, but their glass eyes all seemed to gleam with the same glacial ferocity as Uncle Heinrich's, and they seemed to be crying silently in their several voices: *Victims, victims! As we are, so you shall be....*

My hand sought Charlotte's and squeezed it fiercely. With a sharp smothered cry, she awoke—and sat up, as I had done, and then pressed her hand to her head.

"Lucy! Where are we? Oh! My head—I feel sick—" She sank back on the rug and turned swiftly onto her side, so that I thought for a moment that she was going to *be* sick. But the impulse passed and she relaxed. "Oh, Lucy, my head does hurt...."

"I think we've been drugged, Charlotte. It was the wine."

"Oh, no—poison!"

"No, not poison—just something to make us fall asleep. I don't remember anything after starting to eat—"

"I remember Herr Snivelwurst sneezing all over me, disgusting man....Oh, what are we going to do?"

I sat up, more carefully this time, and looked at the clock. It was nearly half-past eleven. Just over half an hour to midnight....

"Lucy, the time!" said Charlotte. "They should be here by now!"

"Perhaps the clock's fast. I'm sure it's fast. It can't be half-past eleven already." I tried to sound calm.

But she too was on her feet now, peering up at the clock. Just as she did so, it seemed to sense our presence and a spring deep inside its wicked heart began to whirr. We stepped back involuntarily, and the clock struck once for the half-hour and then seemed to sigh with an unpleasant satisfaction as the spring unwound inside it.

"What can we *do?*" Charlotte said.

She ran to the window. I ran to the door. It was locked. The window was barred. There was no way out....We came together in the center of the room, looking this way and that, distracted, nearly mad with fear.

"We've got to think, Charlotte; we mustn't just give up and start wailing—Miss Davenport wouldn't want that. Listen: what about the chimney? Could we climb up through that?"

In a moment we were both on our knees, peering at it. Oh, if only it wasn't so dark—and if only all the shadows weren't so full of horrors. But we felt all round the sooty cavity with our hands, and no, there wasn't room.

It was only a narrow slot in the wall, lined with bricks, not one of those great friendly chimneys you could get right into and sit next to the fire.

What next? Could we break the door down?

No—it was too solid, and there was no furniture, nothing to use as a battering ram, even if we had the strength, which we did not.

The window? Could we slip through the bars?

No—we might break the glass, but the bars were too closely set and newly fixed into the wood. It was then that I saw our uncle's wickedness most clearly. He knew we'd try to escape; he knew he'd have to block every means; and even in a small detail like barring the window, he'd been thorough. I nearly despaired. It seemed that he'd thought of everything. We were helpless.

"Lucy," whispered Charlotte, "what will he do?"

No need to ask who *he* was: Zamiel, of course.

"I don't know, I don't know," I said, so frightened that I sounded angry.

"He'll tear us to pieces!" she said, and her voice was so weak it was almost lost. "The hounds—I've seen what they do—"

"Oh, so have I! Do stop, Charlotte! We'll be all right. Miss Davenport said...."

Charlotte sank to the floor again and drew the blankets over herself. It might have been cold or it might have been terror; I felt both those sensations myself, and was powerfully tempted to join her. But I thought of Miss Davenport, and of Hildi, on her way now to rescue us. I looked out of the window at the grim ranks of pine trees. Even if we could get out, we would be no safer out there.

The clock ticked on. There was a peal of thunder, very far away over the mountains. I was so tense that I heard every sound there was to hear: real ones, like the smug wheeze of the clock, and imaginary ones, like the terrified scramble of small woodland creatures to bury themselves in their burrows out of reach of the Demon Huntsman. Who would be here in—I looked at the hated instrument—a quarter of an hour....

Another peal of thunder. And what was that? Hooves? And that far-off, lost, wailing sound, like the voices of phantom children on the shores of the kingdom of the dead—was that the hounds?

No, no—I was imagining it.

But I wasn't imagining the hoofbeats. They were louder. They were real. I ran to Charlotte and tugged her up, and we clung together, with no words left to speak, as the rider drew up his horse outside. Zamiel? Was it the Demon himself? But it wasn't midnight yet, and the horse was whinnying and stamping the ground as if it was frightened itself.

There was a moment's pause, and then a blow on the door—and then another and another, as if some other demon were seeking to break in and consume us before Zamiel could arrive.

"Hildi!" I cried, more in despair than hope.

But another voice answered—a man's, and we could not hear what he said, for now there was no doubt about it: above his voice sounded the eerie baying of hounds, coming nearer. Charlotte's hands were gripping mine and our eyes were turned toward the door in terror, as the man outside shouted louder and hammered more furiously on the heavy door.

And then, pure and savage and blood-chilling, came the worst sound of all: the single wild note of a hunting horn....

PART THREE

Hildi Again

ONE

I had to keep saying to myself: Peter'll lose the police, he's too clever for them, they'll never find him....Because otherwise, I'd have cried.

It all depended on him. There was nothing I could do. A terrible feeling, that: to see something dreadful happening and to be powerless to help....But as I sat shivering in the darkness and listened to the shouts of pursuit dying away up the road and felt my shoulder and arm begin to throb with pain from where I'd fallen on them, I was conscious of something I'd never known before—and it was so odd that I couldn't put a name to it, at first. I had to search my memory before I came up with the word that fitted. And that word was *vengeance*.

Yes, it was very strange. You read about the *banditti* in Sicily, about their blood feuds and their proud way of avenging their honor, and you think: Well, they're different, those Southerners, they're more passionate than we are. We're a bit stolid here in Switzerland; we don't carry on like that. But then you remember that William Tell was Swiss, and was there ever a braver, prouder action than when he tucked the second arrow into his belt, to use on the hated tyrant Gessler if he'd missed and killed his son with the first? Maybe we're not so dull. Maybe we can be passionate too, if we're stirred. And I was stirred now. I didn't know what I was going to do, but I was going to do something. Count Karlstein was as bad as Gessler—if not worse—and it was time someone told him so. I set off for the castle.

I can't really remember that walk up the mountain. Hardly surprising, I suppose; I'd done it so many times, I could have walked up there with my eyes shut and not fallen over the edge. All I can recall is a sensation as if I had thunder and lightning inside me. Anger; fury. I was hot and cold and dizzy and tired, and I suppose a little crazy by now. It seemed to take no time at all before I was standing outside the castle gate.

I looked up at the tower first, to see if his study window was illuminated. It wasn't. Well, if he wasn't there, I could get there first—and give him a surprise when he did arrive. Very quietly, then, and taking great care to keep in the shadows, I slipped inside the gate and made my way around the edge of the courtyard. One or two of the dogs looked up, and my heart missed a beat, but dogs don't know if you've been dismissed; as far as they were concerned, I still belonged, and when they'd seen who it was, they settled down again.

The castle clock struck as I came to the stable door: eight o'clock. I lifted the latch and went inside, feeling my way along the wall until I came to the door of a little room where I knew they kept things like brushes and saddle soap—and candles. I fumbled through the drawers until I found one and then made my way out and onto the back staircase. It wasn't a route I'd used very often, since my work hadn't taken me to the stables, but I knew it well enough. It was narrow and steep and filthy dirty—and pitch black. There was a small window at every floor, but this was the shadow-side of the castle, and precious little light—and dirty, secondhand light, at that—came in.

Then I had to creep along a corridor under the attics and down another staircase to the hall. This was the riskiest part of the whole journey. I waited, and held my breath, and rushed across to the fire and lit my candle; and then went swiftly under the stone archway that led to the tower and climbed the stairs to the study, guarding the flame from the drafts that streamed like ghostly flags from every crack in the wall. As I climbed, I wondered how long it would take the count to get back through the forest after leaving the girls in the lodge. He'd have Snivelwurst with him and that would slow him down, but they must be fairly close by now. However, he might not come directly up to his study; he'd want to eat first and get warm.

I reached the top floor, the narrow little landing with the lancet window where I'd first heard the horrible plan, and paused. What next? Into the study. I shut the door quickly behind me and looked around with great curiosity, for I'd never been inside it before.

It was a large room that took up the whole of that floor of the tower apart from the landing. In one corner there was a set of wooden steps that led to a trapdoor in the ceiling—obviously the way to the roof. Three of the walls were covered with bookshelves, rank upon rank of dusty leather tomes. In the center of the room there was a desk, littered with papers, and against one wall there was a great oak chest.

A sudden draft swirled around me, and I looked up at the diamond-paned window. It wouldn't be a bad idea to pull the curtains across, I thought. Then I sat in his chair and leaned back. It was a deep, comfortable one, with velvet cushions and wide arms; and I thought, how pleasant to be wealthy, with comfortable chairs and leisure to sit down in them. I began to daydream. And before I knew what was happening, I'd fallen asleep.

I woke suddenly, with a horrible start. The candle had burnt down and gone out, leaving a smoky smell and a little lake of hot wax on the polished leather of the desk top; it must have been the sudden extinguishing of the light that had woken me.

But what a lot of time had gone by! It wasn't dark—quite—because the curtains didn't meet and a crack of moonlight shone through. As I sat bolt upright in the chair, with a beating heart, I heard the castle clock give that sort of ticking whirr that told that it was about to strike. I held my breath. It struck one. How frustrating! Did that mean one o'clock, or half-past something else? I found myself growing rapidly very much more afraid than I'd been earlier.

But I didn't have time to think about that. Voices, from below…

I stood up hastily. All my brave thoughts of vengeance, of confronting him with his own wickedness, had all crept away while I'd been asleep and unable to keep hold of them. Now I was terrified. Where could I hide? That chest beside the steps to the roof—was there any space behind it? There was. I scrambled over the dark oak and lay down flat on the floor—as the door opened and in came the count.

I listened. He wasn't alone; he was talking to someone, but I couldn't hear what he was saying at first. Then he shut the door, and I heard them more clearly.

"Oh, the poet Byron himself couldn't have expressed it better, your grace," said an oily voice—Snivelwurst, of course. "I've always held the opinion that if your grace had turned your talents to the drama, say—" (sneeze)—"or to verse, you would have become the foremost poet of the age.

It is a great pleasure to me to hear you talk, your grace; believe me, it is."

I couldn't see either of them, of course, but I could hear where their voices were coming from. Count Karlstein's came directly toward me as he said, "You're a fool, Snivelwurst." Then something soft dropped over the chest, covering the gap behind it where I crouched and making it dark. It was his cloak. I heard him sniff.

"Something burning? Can you smell that?" he said.

"Alas! I can smell nothing, your grace." (Sneeze.) "But bless my soul! Look here, upon your desk! Someone has been up here with a candle!"

I thought that was the end, that they'd search the room, find me, and fling me in the dungeons, or else shoot me outright. But Count Karlstein merely laughed.

"I expect Frau Muller has found a new parlormaid. About time, too. That slut who broke her foot's just lying up in her room guzzling my food and doing nothing to earn it—and the other one, that girl from the inn, she was no damn good anyway. Clumsy, snooping wench. Give me some brandy, Snivelwurst."

Oh, yes, I thought. I heard the count settle into his armchair and a sound as if he was putting his feet up on the desk. There was the tinkle of glass, the delicate sound of liquid.

"Have one yourself. And bring me a cigar from the humidor," said the count.

"You are very kind, your grace. I should esteem it an honor."

There was a pause then, following which the smell of cigar smoke came faintly to my narrow little hideout.

"You know, Snivelwurst," said the count in a ruminative tone, "I haven't felt safe for—oh, ten years or more. Strange feeling. Don't quite know how to describe it."

"I am fascinated, your grace."

"Mmm. If you take risks, though, you must be prepared for danger....I don't think I'd do it again, mind you."

"What is that, your grace?"

"Make a bargain with...the Prince of Darkness."

"Ah, the—er—bargain...I know it's not my place, Count Karlstein, sir, to ask, as it were, but I must confess to an awesome curiosity, your grace...."

The count laughed harshly. "You want to know what it's all about? Is that it?"

"I should be very honored, your grace...."

"Very well. It's over now, so I may as well tell you. Ten years ago I was a poor man, Snivelwurst. No hope, no prospects—nothing. That was up by the Brocken, in the Harz mountains, up north....I'd been a soldier, you see. Younger son, no estate...my fool of an elder brother inherited everything. So I made a bargain with Zamiel. He was to have—well, you know what *he* was to have; and I was to have a great estate, an honorable name, and wealth.

We signed a document. In blood, Snivelwurst."

I imagined the oily little man shuddering melodramatically; and then the count went on:

"I didn't know what it would mean until a month or so later. My father's estate had been a modest one—little more than a farm. No good to anyone, except my pious brother and his fat wife. Well, Zamiel told me to kill them."

"What!"

"So I did. Set fire to the place, burned them both to cinders. I was the next in line, you see—though what use a pile of ash was, I couldn't see. But then came Zamiel's cleverness. The very next day there came a letter from Geneva, naming the owner of our estate—me, now, you see—as the next in line to the much bigger estate of Karlstein! And here I am. But, as I say, I wouldn't do it again. Not like that; not quite like that."

"I would never have had the courage, Count Karlstein. I take my hat off to you. I salute your daring. A dark and dangerous bargain indeed! Only nerves of steel, only a heart of ice could have carried it through!"

"And there's no risk of that other claimant to the title turning up—the lawyer was plain about that. The estate's mine for good, Snivelwurst. For good! What d'you think of that?"

"You do the title honor by bearing it, your grace."

"Oh, sit down, man, sit down and stop bowing at me," snapped the count wearily.

Another chair scraped across the floor. Count Karlstein continued:

"I shall have to think about marrying next. Ha! Getting an heir! I should have done that years ago, perhaps—but with that bargain hanging over me, well, I don't know...."

"The title's yours for good, your grace," said Snivelwurst again, more quietly this time, trying—as he always did—to match his companion's mood but not sure what that mood was. I shouldn't have liked to guess, either; I'd never heard the count ruminative before. It was an ugly sound: the daydreams of a greedy bear.

"For good," he said slowly. "An odd phrase, isn't it? For good. Well, why not, I wonder?"

"Why not what, your grace?"

"Why not spend the rest of my life—doing good?"

"An extraordinary notion! Most strange!"

"Why's that?" said the count, more sharply—just flicking out his claws to keep Snivelwurst nervous and himself amused.

"Oh! The originality, sir—the, er—unexpectedness," said the secretary lamely.

"Fool. Still, why not? I wonder what it feels like...."

"To do good?" Snivelwurst attempted a light, sophisticated laugh.

"There must be something in it. People don't do anything without getting something from it, Snivelwurst. I admit it seems unlikely now, but there must be some kind of pleasure in it. After all, think of this: d'you like olives?"

"Thank you, your grace—very much—"

"I was asking, fool, not offering! And caviar? D'you like caviar?"

"Delicious, your grace…"

"And did you when you first tasted them?"

"Not at all, sir."

"But you kept on, eh? You saw that others liked them and you thought there must be something in it—eh? And you found that you liked them after all?"

"Exactly it, your grace! A masterly piece of analysis!"

"Well, then, it'll be just the same with doing good."

A little silence. I could imagine Snivelwurst digesting this argument and wondering to himself not about the truth of it but whether the count really believed it, and how it would affect him personally. As for me, I was horrified— more by this even than by the revelation that the count had murdered his own brother. I thought then, and I think still, and I'll go to my grave still thinking, that good should be done for its own sake and for nothing else. The idea that anyone could do good merely as a source of curious pleasure made me feel cold and fearful; because if that pleasure palled, might they not turn just as casually to cruelty instead?

He went on: "There's plenty to be done in the village

here. The people are poor, the houses are falling to pieces, there are old men without work, old women without warm clothes—I could change all that. Change it at once!"

"I suppose you could, your grace," replied Snivelwurst cautiously.

"I could start tomorrow at the shooting contest! An extra prize, eh? A bag of gold, donated by Count Karlstein! Or better still—a banquet for all the villagers! How would they like that? And I'll make a speech and tell them all my plans."

"Plans, your grace? Already?"

"Give me some more brandy, man—yes, plans. Easy. I'll build a hospital! How's that?"

"Very generous! Magnificent!"

"New roofs on all the village houses—"

"Capital, capital!"

"New shoes for all the children—"

"Sublime! Incomparable!"

"A new bell for the church—almshouses for the aged— a drinking-trough for horses—"

"Peerless! Unparalleled!"

"Ah, Snivelwurst! This is a novel experience! Being good…I can see that it could last a lifetime, this business. I could do so much! I wonder.…" His voice trailed away as he considered his future saintliness, and in the wide silence I could hear, far below, as it seemed, the great mechanism of the castle clock beginning to stir itself once again. It had struck once last time: what would it strike now?

One...two...

"When I die," said the count—

...three...four...five...

—"all the little children will shed tears—"

...six...seven...

—"and they'll shut the village school for a day—"

...eight...nine...

—"and all the children will come to the castle—"

...ten...eleven...

—"each carrying a posy of flowers—for good Count Karlstein!"

...twelve....

Midnight!

Far away in the forest—what was happening? Oh, what was happening? This was the hour that Zamiel had named! And—

Very soft, very faint—as soft and faint as the dream of a memory of a dream—there came into the silence the note of a hunting horn.

"What was that?" Count Karlstein's voice—tense, all at once.

And the horn sounded again. Not a bright, cheerful note with sunshine and fresh air and the dappled leaves of the forest in it; something wilder, colder, far more terrible. The horn of Zamiel!

I heard the secretary scuttle across the floor and draw the curtain.

"Leave it, fool!" snarled the count.

"But I heard—"

"Hush!" said Count Karlstein.

And again—but closer now, only a league or two distant, perhaps, and so high up it could only have come from the bare chilly wilderness of the sky itself—again, the horn. And a rumble, like the first mutter of thunder: hoofbeats?

"Zamiel," said the count, and there was horror in his voice. "Surely not…It's my heart, how it's racing! Come here, Snivelwurst, put your hand on my chest, feel my heart—can you feel it? Can you feel it racing?"

"Oh, indeed, beating like a drum, your grace. That's what it is—not a shadow of doubt. Best lie down, Count Karlstein—a glass of brandy—"

"What's the matter with me?" said the count, and now there was an angry puzzlement in his voice. "Calm down! Stop panicking—control yourself…there's nothing wrong…."

I'd twisted round, so that by lifting up the count's cloak just a little I could see from beneath it. Snivelwurst was helping him to the chair, looking white in the face himself. But the count looked dreadful; his face was suffused with darkness, his eyes stared wildly, his hands clutched convulsively at the arms of the chair—and I swear I could see his hair bristling on the top of his head. I've never seen such a picture of mortal fear; it made my skin crawl.

And outside…

The count flung Snivelwurst aside, and the little rat-like man fell to the floor, twisting as he fell, and wriggled out of reach. Count Karlstein rose from the chair and rushed to the window, shielding his face, and then turned aside swiftly and stood with his back pressed against the wall.

"After all, he's bound to make some sort of noise…" he said, quickly and almost under his breath, as if he was trying to reassure himself. "He wouldn't hunt silently, would he…? But why come this way? Surely he should go back to the Brocken, when he's hunted? He must have found them now—it's after midnight—"

A thin, wild howling, like that of some creature composed only of ferocious greed, came through the tense air like a needle. The hounds! He heard it, and seemed to crumple suddenly, as if a huge invisible hand had reached inside his breast and crushed his heart. He sank back against the tapestry and put up one hand. His face was the color of a thundercloud—like a bruise, purple and angry black; and I thought: Is he going to have a stroke? And one eye (I saw with horror) had suddenly become so shot with blood that it looked as if blood was going to spill out like a cascade of scarlet tears.

"No, no—I'm imagining it! It's not Zamiel now—it's after midnight—He hasn't come for me? Not for *me!* I've given him his victims, haven't I? No, no!"

There was a bubbling, whining sound from the table, and I tore my eyes away from the dreadful spectacle of the count to see Snivelwurst, his knees knocking together, attempting to pull the tablecloth over himself in the last extremity of terror.

The hounds—again, and much, much closer! And cries from no human throat—and hoofbeats more thunderous than any that trod the good earth—and the crack of a whip that sounded as long and as vicious as a tongue of lightning. The air outside the tower was full of it now: the Wild Hunt itself, careering closer—the hounds in full cry, the air and the stone echoing, trembling, shaking with the awesome force of it. I said a prayer. The count clung to the tapestry and cried:

"No, no! Not me! I'm good! I've just decided to be good! *I've repented!*"

And then a voice as deep as the roots of the mountains, as majestic as the thunder that plays between them, said:

"Too late!"

The glass in the window shook; the flame of the candle flared and streamed, and the tapestries lifted themselves off the walls as if a mighty wind had blown straight through the stone. Count Karlstein staggered.

"No, no"—he cried—"it's never too late!"

"*Too late! Midnight has come and gone. Where is my prey?*"

"At the hunting lodge. I locked them in—I swear I did!"

And again the voice cried: "*Too late! Too late!*"

"No—no—"

"*For ten years I have waited for this night. Where is my prey?*"

"I took them there myself! I locked the door!"

"*The hunting lodge was empty, Heinrich Karlstein.*"

"I don't believe it! No—it isn't possible!"

A gust of wind more powerful, I swear, than any that had beaten against the stone of the tower for a thousand years or more seized it and shook it from side to side as a young tree can be shaken by a man's fist. Count Karlstein fell to his knees, and his eyes—one full of blood, the other so wide with fear that I thought it would burst from his head—rolled this way and that, seeking safety.

But there was none. For once again the great voice of the Demon Hunter—sonorous as a mighty organ, yet with depths of jagged harshness, discordant tones of mockery in it—filled the small room, washing through it as a wave on the stormy sea would sweep through the length of a smashed and drifting boat.

"*It is after midnight now, Count Karlstein.*"

"No, no! I beg you!"

"Ten years ago we made a bargain. Now I have come to col-
lect what is due to me...."

"No—no—"

And the glass of the window burst, and the heavy curtains rose up and drew together like gigantic hands—and
then they were not curtains anymore, nor hands, but a bil-
lowing cloak, fastened at the neck with a clasp of blazing
fire. And the great Being who wore the cloak had no face,
nor body, nor arms, nor legs, but was composed all of
impenetrable Darkness. And the Darkness laughed, and the
room was filled with the baying of hounds; and the sounds
and the Darkness flung themselves at Count Karlstein, and
took him up and crushed him like a piece of paper and
dropped him to the floor—dead.

As for what happened then, I have no knowledge at all,
because I fainted clean away. But when I woke up—and it
can't have been more than a minute or two later—the candle had blown out and only the moonlight illuminated the
room, in a wide swathe of cool silver from the broken window (the curtains hanging, torn and ragged, on either side)
to the overturned table. Count Karlstein lay, face down—
thank Heaven!—in the center, and the secretary had fled.
Some distant swirl of sound that might well have been my
imagination diminished in the distant sky. Otherwise,
everything was silent.

I stood up, trembling, and felt my way to the door. After

what I'd seen, I had no fear of the castle servants, and I ran down the stairs quite openly. The great hall was deserted; the fire was burning low and its embers gave the only light. I looked around for a lamp or a candle that I might light from the last coals and then I heard voices, high-pitched, panicking, and looked up to see who it was.

Frau Muller closely followed by Snivelwurst scuttled into the hall like a pair of seedy mice. She was wearing a dressing gown and a nightcap, and carrying a carpetbag— and something seemed to have happened to her face: it had sunk, and her nose and chin had grown closer together. She looked mad, quite deranged, like an inhabitant of Bedlam. She saw me and shrieked and mumbled, pointing angrily— and then I saw that she'd got no teeth. False teeth! I never knew that! She must have left them beside her bed....At any rate, she held her dressing gown away from me and fled. And Snivelwurst...I think, of all the things I've ever seen, that was the strangest and the most pathetic. For whether you liked him or loathed him, he was a grown man; and yet he hastened after her, whimpering with fear, and tried to hold her hand....

They dragged the great door wide and vanished through it; and that was the last I saw of them.

TWO

Sunshine, birdsong, the sparkling river, with a blue sky above it all—you'd have thought there was no such being as Zamiel, no such thing as darkness, no such time as midnight. The village looked its very best. The dew—it had been frost a little earlier, but the sun had been at it—gave the stone of the bridge and the houses all the brightness of fresh paint, and the air was tingling just like the water they bottle in Andersbad, further down the valley.

I'd left Frau Wenzel the cook in charge at the castle. She'd heard the terrible sounds from the tower, and she and little Susi Dettweiler, and Johann and Adolphus, were shivering in the kitchen when I came down; and now that Frau Muller and Snivelwurst had disappeared, it was obvious that the old cook was in charge.

But I couldn't stay there. I had to know what had happened to the girls, and it was in the village that we'd agreed to meet, if everything had gone according to Miss Davenport's plan. Besides, this was the day of the shooting contest. And there was Peter to think about....I was trembling with impatience and curiosity.

But here was the village green, with no one about as yet; and here was the Jolly Huntsman, with old Conrad swilling down the front step with a bucket and mop, though it was so clean already that you could have eaten your breakfast off it. Breakfast! I nearly fell over with hunger as I thought of it.

"Where've you been to?" said old Conrad, stepping down to make room for me to go in. "You mind this step, now. Lift that skirt up—don't trail it in the water. You're all muddy and dirty. Where've you been?"

"Here and there," I said. "Has Peter come back yet?"

He frowned and looked around, and put his finger to his lips, and I remembered that Peter was still an outlaw. "I don't know anything about that," he muttered. "He's a wild one, that boy."

The clock on the church struck seven.

"Isn't there anyone about?" I said. "Are they all still in bed?"

"Where was you last night, then? Didn't you hear all that to-do up yonder?"

"Where was that?" I said innocently.

"All Souls' Eve, last night, it was. You be thankful you

was out of it, my girl. You don't want to go wandering about on All Souls' Eve—you want to stay indoors and say your prayers."

"Well, I'm here now. Is Ma up? She's surely not still in bed?"

"You know your ma better than that. You'd better go and give her a hand—she's got a houseful of guests to feed. I don't know what you're coming to—getting dismissed from a good position like what you had up there, and then wandering about all night. You'll be the death of her, you will, you and that rascal of a brother...."

I left him to his grumbling and hurried to the kitchen. Ma was stirring some eggs in a big pan, and Hannerl was heating some water for coffee. As soon as they saw me, they each gave a little cry, dropped what they were doing, and ran to me. I felt oddly embarrassed.

"Oh, Hildi, darling! You're safe! Thank God, thank God!"

That was Ma, pressing me to her breast and nearly stifling me. And Hannerl clasped her hands and just looked at me, with a big dumb question in her big blue eyes—and I had to shrug, as best I could in that soft imprisonment.

"He hasn't come back yet, then?" I said as soon as she set me free.

"You haven't seen him either?" said Ma, and her expression was all anxiety.

I shook my head. "He'll be back before long," I said. "And he'll want a big breakfast, too."

"Oh, Lord—the eggs," said Ma, and rushed to the fire, just in time to save them from a scorching doom.

"D'you think he's safe, Hildi?" said Hannerl.

"I know he is. I don't know where he is now, but I know he's not...." I trailed off, not wanting to say *dead*. But did I know? I'd heard the terrible voice of the Demon say that the hunting lodge was empty, but what did that prove? He might have enjoyed his first helping so much that he'd come back for another. I just spread my hands, and Hannerl sniffed and blinked before going back to her work.

I thought: Shall I tell them about last night? And then I thought: No, I can't; it's not the time for it. Besides, I wanted to forget it, if I could—it was too dark, too overwhelming. So I joined in with the cooking. This must have been the biggest breakfast the Jolly Huntsman had ever served—the place was bursting. And all the familiarity of the dishes, the cutlery, the warm, friendly smells and sounds seemed to bathe away the bad memories of the night like a warm bath. Hannerl and I served the breakfast and washed the dishes, and got it done quickly, since there were two of us; though most of the guests weren't in any frame of mind to linger. They all had their minds on the contest.

As soon as I could, I went out to see what was going on. The contest was to be held on the village green; and there were a couple of men there already, putting up a platform for the Mayor, with a striped awning over it. I stood and watched them for a minute and then walked on. I couldn't help it; I was nervous. Nervous for Peter, for Frau Wenzel and Susi (would Frau Muller and the secretary come back?) and, most of all, nervous for Lucy and Charlotte.

But the first people on the green, apart from the workmen and myself, were none other than Max and Eliza. I didn't notice them at first; they were sitting under the trees, and looking mighty despondent. I rushed up and greeted them, and a pair of long faces turned to look up at me.

"What happened last night?" they said, so I had to go through the whole tale and they oohed and aahed in all the right places. But *they* hadn't seen the girls or Peter either, so when I'd finished, I sat down on the bench beside them and began to share some of their gloom.

"We're in a fine old pickle, Eliza, me love," said Max.

"It's awful, Max!" she said. "Your master arrested, and—"

"I'd forgotten about him," I said.

"'Tis the injustice of fate, Hildi, that's what it is," he said. "Everything happens at once, and all of it's bad."

"I'm sure Miss Davenport'll never come back," said Eliza miserably.

"Why ever not?" I said.

"I had a strange feeling as she left yesterday," she said.

"It was a kind of a galloping feeling in my heart. I used to have a little kitten once, and I had this galloping feeling one day, and three weeks later the kitten was dead. It just died, just like that, under mysterious circumstances. I'm sure Miss Davenport will have fallen over the edge of a cliff...."

"Well, wherever she is, I've got hardly any money left," said Max, in the depths of gloom. "There's nothing for it, my lamb—we'll have to part. I can't marry you now. I can't ask you to share the life of a pauper."

"Move over, mate, you can't sit there," said another voice from behind us.

We looked around, and saw old Gunther the baker, carrying some complicated apparatus made of wood. He nodded at me importantly.

"What's that?" I said.

"This is the target!" he said. "For the contest! It's going to stand right here. You don't want to get shot, do you?"

"It's not such a bad idea," said Max, and he sounded so mournful that I couldn't help laughing.

"What's the prize?" asked Eliza.

"Fifty gold crowns," said Gunther, setting his wooden structure on the ground and unbolting various bits and pieces, "and the title of Chief Ranger of the Forest. It's a great honor, that is."

"Maxie, you ought to enter! You might win!" said Eliza.

"That's all very well, but I ain't got a musket—remember?"

"Oh, no, I'd forgotten," she said sadly. "That's the end of that, then."

We moved aside to let Gunther get on with setting the target up.

"I wonder what'll happen to them kids, when they come back," said Max after a moment.

"There's no one to look after 'em," said Eliza. "They'll be taken into the care of the court, I expect."

"Orphans, are they?" said Max. "Just like me. I was a foundling, too. I didn't have no family to grow up with. Poor little things—they've been through a lot, they have. If I could win that contest…Oh, well, never mind. I ain't got a musket, so that's the end of it."

Suddenly Eliza jumped and squealed, as if she'd been stung by a wasp, and shook his arm.

"Maxie!" she cried.

"What is it?"

"Maxie, your trombone!"

"It ain't a trombone, Eliza, it's a coach-horn—"

But Eliza was already turning away and speaking eagerly to old Gunther.

"Excuse me, sir," she said, curtsying prettily so that he stopped what he was doing and looked at her with interest, "could you tell me what the rules are for the shooting contest, please?"

"Certainly, me dear!" he said. "See this little straw with

the feather in it? Well, that's connected to this bit here, that joins on to the spring underneath, and—well, they have to hit the target smack in the middle, and that makes the feather fly into the air. That's all. But it ain't as easy as it looks."

"They all shoot in turn, do they?" said Max.

"Aye. But as soon as the target's hit, that's the end of the contest. Maybe the first man'll hit it. Maybe no one will—then they'll have to shoot again."

"And does it have to be a musket?" said Eliza.

"Musket, pistol, cannon, whatever you like," he said.

"There, Maxie," she said, in triumph, turning back to him. "Remember how Miss Davenport showed you how to fire your trombone?"

"It ain't a trombone, Eliza, it's a—" He stopped, as he suddenly realized what she meant. "No, I couldn't," he said. "Surely not? I wonder, though—I'd have to go and practice. But no, I couldn't...."

I didn't know what they were talking about; but didn't have time to ask, because at that very moment two small figures wandered around the corner of the Mayor's house and stood, bemused, looking around as if for someone they knew.

"Miss Lucy!" I cried. "Miss Charlotte!"

They ran, and I ran, and Max and Eliza came after me, and we all met in the middle somewhere. The green was filling up now, and people looked at us curiously—and no wonder, because we might, from our exuberance, have been welcoming each other back from the grave. And perhaps (a chilly thought that came and went in a moment) we were.

"You're safe!" I cried, and Eliza said, "What happened?" and Max said, "You're all right, then?" all at once; and Lucy said, "Peter got there just in time!" and Charlotte said, "Oh, it was awful—you'd never believe it. We thought we were lost for ever—" And by the time we'd got those first words out, I'd noticed, and Eliza had noticed too, that the girls were wet through and shivering and worn out. So I made them come with me back to the Jolly Huntsman, to sit by the fire and have something to eat and drink. Ma fussed over them, and I let her, because they needed it; and Max and Eliza sat there, open-mouthed, as Lucy told what had happened in the hunting lodge.

But first—where was Peter? Safe, it seemed, and Hannerl's face grinned seemingly of its own accord, because she couldn't control it at all. He was waiting out of sight for the time being, until the shooting began; he'd take his chance then, but he didn't want to run the risk of being spotted and caught before he'd even had a try at the target.

And while Charlotte sipped some hot milk and yawned and nodded, steaming like a pudding in front of the fire, Lucy explained how Peter had rescued them.

It had been just before midnight when he'd arrived, and

217

they'd thought his volley of knocking on the door was the Demon himself. The door was locked, of course, and he'd had to shoot through the lock to break in. They'd all run out and taken shelter a little way off, there being no time to put more distance between themselves and the lodge, and at five minutes to midnight…the Hunt arrived. Neither of them could describe it properly. But they were certain of one thing, and that was that Peter hadn't fired his musket at all, apart from when he shot through the lock.

"But how did you escape him, then?" I said.

"Oh, it was terrifying!" said Lucy. "Zamiel's horse was huge—halfway up the sky—and all the hounds, you could hear them straining at the leash and foaming and growling—and then Peter just stood up straight and called to Zamiel."

"He did what?"

"He called out!" said Charlotte. "He said, *You're not having these girls! Count Karlstein is your prey—go and seek him!*"

Lucy said, "And Zamiel said, *Who are you?* His voice was like thunder—"

Charlotte said, "And Peter said, Peter Kelmar, a free-born huntsman."

Lucy said, "And Zamiel said, *A huntsman? I do not harm true huntsmen, or those they protect. Go in peace!*"

Charlotte said, "And then Zamiel wheeled his horse around and the hunt rose up into the sky and they all flew away...."

"And do you know?" said Lucy. "Peter only had one bullet with him—and that was the silver one! And he'd shot that through the door letting us out!"

"Oh, the fool," I said. "What was he thinking of?"

"No, he's not!" said Charlotte. "He was really brave."

"That was the bravest thing I ever saw, when he stood up to Zamiel," said Lucy. "If he hadn't done that..."

"Where is he now?" said Hannerl. "Has he still got the horse with him?"

Charlotte explained where Peter was hiding, and Hannerl hastened out. She'd bring the horse back to the stable, she said, since Peter'd be too busy and the owner would be worried about it.

Eliza sat back thoughtfully. "What are you going to do now, though?" she said. "I suppose Miss Davenport could take you in—I know she'd like to, but the law's very strict about that sort of thing."

"It's got to be relations or nothing, that's the law," said Max. "You got any cousins anywhere?"

"No one," said Lucy. "Count Karlstein's our only relative."

"Was," I said, before I could help it. They looked at me in surprise; and I told them, in my turn, what had happened just after midnight in the tower. I missed out some of it, though—I said that their uncle had had an apoplectic fit and died at once. They listened without speaking, without moving, without taking their eyes from my face. And when I'd finished, they said nothing, but looked down at the floor; and Lucy said in a small voice, "We *are* alone, then."

"Oh, nonsense!" said Ma loudly. "You'll always have a welcome here, my dears! You don't think we'd turn you out and wave good-bye, do you?"

"It ain't as simple as that, ma'am, begging your pardon," said Max. "See, being an orphan meself, and in the profession, like, I know a bit about it. If there's no relations living, they'll have to go into an orphanage. That's the law. But they ain't bad places," he went on, turning to the girls. "We had a rare old time in Geneva when I was a lad. We used to play 'em up something terrible, those old biddies who ran the place. There was one time—"

"Hush, Maxie," said Eliza. "We'll think about all that later. When's this contest going to start?" she asked Ma, trying to sound bright and cheery, and not really succeeding. Lucy had tears in her eyes, but she blinked them back and pretended to be interested in the contest, too, and Charlotte was too tired to feel anything.

"Oh!" said Max suddenly. "Begging your pardon, ma'am, but have you got such a thing as a dried pea?"

And that broke the tension and made us laugh, and Ma

said of course she had and how many did he want? And he said, just one, thank you very much, which sounded even odder. So she fetched it for him, and he tried to pay for it but she wouldn't take anything—how can you take money for one dried pea?—and then we all seemed to be getting ready to go out.

The green was full now. The platform was up, the awning was in place, and all the villagers—all who weren't shooting, anyway—seemed to have come. You could hardly move. But the workmen had set up a railing and a rope to hold the audience back from the shooting area, and those men who were competing were strolling about in a lordly manner in front of the platform, watched by all the rest. They loved being watched, too. They held their muskets to their shoulders and sighted along the barrel; they held them in one hand and tested the balance, as if they didn't know the feel of it by heart already; they rolled ball after ball in the palm of their hand, trying to find the most perfect one, the one that would fly straight to the target and win for them. But there was no sign of Peter anywhere; and what on earth was Max doing? He was trying to fit the pea into the mouthpiece of his coach-horn—and then it rolled all the way through and fell out into the grass, and we had to go down on our knees and look for it.

"This is no good, Eliza," he said despondently. "I'll never win like this."

"Don't give up, my love," she said. "Here it is, look!"

Then Lucy grabbed my arm. "Look!" she said. "Doctor Cadaverezzi!"

For into the shooting area in front of the platform came the great genius himself—in chains! On one side of him was Constable Winkelburg and on the other Sergeant Snitsch. Many of the spectators, and the contestants as well, had seen his performance in the Jolly Huntsman, and they cheered and clapped to see him again. He turned and tried to bow, but the policemen hustled him forward. Then Lucy ducked under the rope and ran up to him.

"Doctor Cadaverezzi! What's happening? What are they doing?" she said.

"Princess Nephthys!" he replied, and he did bow this time—a great sweeping gracious bow that had the sergeant and the constable bending too, to avoid letting go, so that they looked like three councillors of state bowing to a little princess. "How enchanting to see you, my dear! I regret that I cannot receive you in the style that I would wish, but—"

"You clear off," said the sergeant to Lucy, "else I'll arrest you and all."

"Sergeant," said Doctor Cadaverezzi, "may I make a last request?"

Everyone's eyes were on him now. He knew how to hold an audience, all right; it's partly skill, I suppose, and partly a sort of godlike cheek.

"A last request?" said the sergeant. "This ain't an execution."

"No?" Doctor Cadaverezzi looked around in surprise. "I saw all the muskets, and I thought—but never mind. One day I shall have the chance to escape a firing squad at the last moment...or better still, the guillotine! Ah, what a spectacle that would make! But who is that? My good Max! Are you prospering?"

"No, I ain't, Doctor, and that's a fact—"

"Come on, cut it out," said the sergeant. "You're under guard, my man. We've got a long way to go this morning."

"Can't he stop and watch the shooting contest?" said Max.

"Yes, let him watch!" came a voice from the crowd, and others joined in too: "He won't escape! Let him watch, go on!"

"Go on, Sarge," said Constable Winkelburg, greatly daring. "I wouldn't mind watching it meself."

"Hmm," said the sergeant. "Very well. But mind you keep a grip on him. He's as slippery as a serpent."

"Thank you, gentlemen," said Doctor Cadaverezzi, bowing again—to the crowd this time. They cheered as the policemen led him to the edge of the platform, and I saw him give a great wink to Lucy.

And then there was a trumpet call and the audience parted to let the officials through.

"Maxie!" said Eliza anxiously. "You haven't had time to practice on your trombone!"

"It ain't a trombone, Eliza," he said, "it's a—oh, never mind. I'll just have to do me best."

And up onto the platform stepped the Mayor, a little plump man called Herr Kessel, and Frau Kessel, his wife, and half a dozen men all dressed in their best, including one wrinkled old huntsman whom I recognized as the man who'd taught Peter to shoot.

"Who's he?" whispered Eliza.

"Herr Stanger," I said. "I think he's the referee."

The Mayor stepped forward and began to speak.

"Ladies and gentlemen! I welcome you on behalf of the Municipal Corporation, and Frau Kessel, and Kessel's Dry Goods Store, to the Grand Shooting Contest, held to determine which of these crack shots, what have assembled here from all parts of the valley and beyond, is the crackest."

Here he paused for breath, and Charlotte craned upward to see better. There was a stir over at the other side of the crowd, beside the Jolly Huntsman; was that someone else arriving? A coach? It was hard to see, and in any case the Mayor was talking again, having taken a deep breath.

"We are deeply privileged to have with us as official on this occasion one whose exploits with the musket have earned our admiration over many years. I refer, of course, to Herr Josef Stanger, to whom I hand you over now, the referee of this noble contest."

The wrinkled old huntsman, blinking a little and on his very best behavior for this large crowd, came forward.

"Good morning, ladies and gentlemen," he said. "Since we don't hold this contest very often, I shall have to remind you of the rules before we start. Every contestant's name goes into the hat, and they shoot in the order in which they are drawn out by His Worship the Mayor. One shot only, and—"

"Hang on!" That was Max, struggling forward.

"What is it?" said the referee, bending down to see what the matter was.

"Is it too late to enter?"

"No," said the referee. "Just write your name on here and give it in."

Max scribbled on the card the referee handed him, while Herr Stanger explained the rest of the rules. Max ducked under the rope and Eliza blew him a kiss. I thought: They'll never let him! But Lucy and Charlotte were waving, too. Max rubbed his hands and shaded his eyes to look at the target.

"Right!" said the referee. "And now, if His Worship will be so kind…"

One of the officials held out a cocked hat to Herr

Kessel, and he dipped a fat little hand into it and handed a card to the referee.

"The first man to shoot is…Adolf Brandt," said Herr Stanger.

One of the contestants called out, "That's me, sir!" and stepped forward and took aim. He fired, and the noise echoed all round the green, but the target didn't budge. The marksman stepped away, disappointed; so much hanging on just one shot! But now the next man was shooting—and with the same result. The third name to come out of the hat was that of Rudi Gallmeyer from the village, and a cheer went up as he came to take his place and shoot; but he too missed.

"It must be harder than it looks," said Lucy.

Another two names were called, another two shots echoed round the green, another two disappointed marksmen went back to join their fellows. Then:

"Max Grindoff," called the referee.

"Ooh! Maxie! It's you!" cried Eliza, and Lucy and Charlotte shouted, "Good luck!"

Max stepped forward. The spectators could see that he had no musket, and there was a buzz of surprise as he shaded his eyes to look hard at the target, put something (the dried pea, I suppose) in his mouth, and then set the long shiny coach-horn to his lips. He took a great lungful of breath.

"Just a minute," said the referee. "What's all this?"

Max put the coach-horn down. "It's a blowpipe," he said. "From Brazil."

Herr Kessel the Mayor came to the edge of the platform and looked down his nose in disapproval. "I can't have that," he said. "It's against all the dignity of the contest."

Herr Stanger the referee shook his head dubiously. Eliza, beside me, was biting her lip in suspense.

"I'm not sure," said the old huntsman. "There's nothing in the rules that says he can't, Your Worship. We've never had a case like this before."

Max was looking more and more unhappy. He looked at the referee and I could tell what he was thinking. He spat out the pea and put the coach-horn down. "No," he said, "the Mayor's right. This contest is too ancient and noble to be won by a peashooter; it wouldn't be right."

"You wouldn't win anyway," said the Mayor scornfully, "blowing that ridiculous trombone."

This was too much for Eliza. "It ain't a trombone, Mr. Mayor," she said with great dignity, "it's a coach-pipe."

"Eh?" said the Mayor.

"No! Sorry! I mean, it ain't a trompipe, it's a coach-bone. No! I mean—"

"Never mind, Eliza, give it up," said Max. The audience was following this with great interest; they'd taken a liking to Max and they approved of his respect for their traditions.

He turned to them. "The fact is, gents," he said, "I ain't got a musket, owing to me britches catching fire—what I won't go into now—but I withdraw from this contest, not wanting to undignify it, like."

"Good for you, mate!" came a voice from the crowd.

"Lend him a musket—go on," suggested another.

The other competitors nodded in agreement, and Rudi Gallmeyer loaded his musket and handed it to Max, who bowed to them all.

"Gentlemen," he said, "that does you very proud. I takes my hat off to you—sportsmen, every one. Here we go, then!" He raised the musket, took aim—and what happened next isn't easy to describe.

I think, first of all, that he must have trodden on a stone and turned his foot, because he seemed to slip sideways suddenly, and as he fell, he must have pulled the trigger; and the musket was swinging wildly through the air, so his aim wasn't quite where it might have been. In fact, the bullet went straight into the Mayor's hat, and that noble piece of headgear flew off the municipal head as if Doctor Cadaverezzi had put a spring in it. The Mayor clapped his hand to his bare pate with an expression of outraged amazement, which quickly turned to apprehension, for that magnificent bullet hadn't finished yet. The next thing it did was to sever one of the ropes that held the awning up—and a great sheet of stripy canvas descended gracefully over the Mayor's wife, who disappeared with a faint shriek.

And attached to the canvas was a stout pole, which swung down and rapped Constable Winkelburg smartly on the helmet. With a squeal of terror, he staggered forward and grabbed at the first thing he could find, to save himself. And the first thing he could find was Sergeant Snitsch's trousers.

They came down like an avalanche of blue serge. It was a majestic sight; and underneath them, he was wearing a pair of enormous drawers made of some stripy material that looked exactly like the stuff the Mayor's wife, still shrieking, was threshing and heaving and struggling to get out of.

That took less time to happen than it does to describe. In one moment, the place was in chaos. There was a second or two's awed silence, as the audience tried to take in what had happened—and then, as one man, they turned to the creator of it all, the incomparable Max, and cheered him to the echo. They laughed, they clapped, they roared their approval—and the most enthusiastic applause of all came from Doctor Cadaverezzi.

"Bravo!" he cried. "Bravissimo! What brilliant shooting, Max!"

The best thing of all was Max's face. He stood there quite awestruck, scratching his head with amazement as the chaos and the laughter spread. "Well, I'm blowed," he said at last. "How did that happen?"

"I'm afraid you missed the target," said the referee, trying to look serious so as not to offend the Mayor.

"Oh, was that it?" said Max. "Well, thanks for the musket, mate." He handed it back, and came to lean against the barrier where we were standing, while the officials replaced the awning and the Mayor untangled his wife and Sergeant Snitsch retired behind the platform to attend to his trousers. The constable (dazed) and Doctor Cadaverezzi (beaming) had to go with him, as they were all chained together.

And as the next contestant took his place, there came a familiar voice from behind us.

"Good morning, girls!"

They turned in delight.

"Miss Davenport!" said Lucy.

"Oh, thank goodness—" said Charlotte, and then broke off, and curtsied to the old gentleman who stood behind Miss Davenport. He bowed just as politely in return, to the both of them, and I recognized the lawyer, Meister Haifisch, that cool old skeleton who'd come to see Count Karlstein (and it seemed like weeks ago, instead of three or four days).

Miss Davenport could see that we were all bursting with questions. She held up her hand.

"Do not let us interrupt the contest," she said. "Lucy, your hair is remarkably disordered; and Charlotte, you have not washed your face since the day before yesterday; but otherwise you look quite well, quite well indeed. I am delighted to see you. But let us be quiet. The referee is about to call another contestant."

The Mayor took a card from the hat and handed it to Herr Stanger.

"Peter Kelmar," he called.

I gasped. Peter at last—and he wasn't there! I could sense Ma, behind me, and Hannerl, too, biting their lips and clasping their hands with suspense; and I felt my heart beat a good deal faster, too.

"There he is!" cried Lucy, pointing.

And there he was, strolling around the edge of the platform as cool as you please. At least, he looked cool—and to the spectators, he must have looked downright arrogant. But I knew he'd be strung up as tight as a violin string, and I only hoped the danger and exhaustion of the night hadn't unsettled whatever steadiness he'd been able to build into himself during his time in the cellar. He came to the mark— I crossed my fingers—he raised the musket—I held my breath—and then there came an interruption.

Sergeant Snitsch, one hand on his trousers and the other brandishing a truncheon, rushed out from behind the platform.

"Stop!" he cried. "Peter Kelmar, you're under arrest! There's a price on your head, young man!"

Peter stood quite still for a moment, and then lowered the musket carefully before looking around. What he'd have done next, I don't know; but it was the referee who spoke.

"No," he said firmly. "I can't have that. While he's taking part in the contest, he must be a free man, since it says in the rules that only free men can take part."

Sergeant Snitsch was astonished. "But I've arrested him!" he said.

"Oh, no, you haven't," said Herr Stanger, "because he'd already started. He's a free man!"

The audience, thanks to Max, was in a good mood and they cheered at this verdict. Sergeant Snitsch had to back down.

"Only till he shoots," he grumbled. "I'll have him then."

"That's up to you, Sergeant," said the referee. "Now, stand aside, if you please."

The sergeant tucked his truncheon under his arm and stood out of the way, fixing his trousers. The audience fell still, and Peter lifted his musket for the second time.

You remember what I said about William Tell? Well, that came back to me again. For Peter wasn't shooting only for the prize; he was shooting for his freedom, and all the spectators knew it. I'd have shaken like a leaf; most people would. But that's the difference between you and me, on the one hand, and a champion, on the other. For he held the musket as still and steady as a stone carving, and then he squeezed the trigger; and just as if it had been rehearsed, the feather flew high into the air.

He'd hit the target! He'd won!

It took a moment or two for the audience to realize—and then such a cheer broke out as I'd never heard in my life. They threw their hats in the air, they slapped each other on the back, they laughed and shouted and cheered with joy.

And then the sergeant stepped forward again, and the noise died away. "Right, my lad," he said with satisfaction, "I've got you now."

"Just a minute," said Peter. "Haven't I won the contest, Herr Stanger?"

"You have," said the referee.

"So I'm Chief Ranger of the Forest?"

"That's right," said Herr Stanger, nodding briskly.

"So what?" said Sergeant Snitsch.

"So he's a free man, that's what," said Herr Stanger loudly, "since only a free man can be Chief Ranger of the Forest!"

And if the first cheer was loud, this was louder still. Hannerl was jumping up and down, Ma was wringing her hands and trying to clap them at the same time, Lucy and Charlotte were cheering, and I thought the awning was going to fall again through being shaken loose by the noise.

Peter stepped up and shook the Mayor's hand and was presented with a scroll and a bag of gold, and bowed very respectfully to the Mayor's wife. You'd never have thought he'd been a desperate criminal, wanted by the police, only five minutes before.

And that, I suppose, would have been that; we'd all have gone home and had lunch, and the excitement would have been over. But there was Miss Davenport—and what was she doing? Ducking under the ropes, holding up her hand for silence, standing on the steps of the platform?

"Your Worship," she said in her best classroom voice: loud, clear, and wake-up-at-the-back-there. "Ladies and gentlemen, I have an important announcement to make. I do not like to mar your joy on this happy occasion with somber thoughts, but I have to tell you that Heinrich, Count Karlstein, is no more."

Even those in the audience who didn't know who Count Karlstein was—the visitors, those from the other valleys—gathered from the stunned silence that he was someone of importance. And they'd have gathered from the odd quality of the silence—interested more than sorrowful—that he wasn't wholly loved by those who did know him. Miss Davenport went on:

"As this is an event which concerns you all, I thought it best to announce it now. I call to witness Meister Haifisch."

The lawyer (everyone could see he was a lawyer; something in the dry, actorish way he took the center of the platform, I expect) bowed to the Mayor, the referee, the Mayor's wife, and finally Peter (who bowed back with all the authority of his new rank), and spoke.

"The body of Count Karlstein was discovered this morning by one of his servants. He had suffered an apoplectic fit during the night. The question of the Karlstein estate is a very unusual one, which may excuse our dealing with it in this unusual way. To begin with, there are his two nieces—Miss Lucy and Miss Charlotte."

"Oh!" gasped Eliza. Charlotte's hand crept into mine; what was going to happen?

"As these two young ladies are without living relatives," the lawyer continued in his precise, cool way, "they are declared wards of court and taken into custody."

Charlotte gave a little cry. Lucy took her hand and the two of them shrank together, a little apart from the rest of us. We watched helplessly.

"However," Meister Haifisch went on, "there is a complication. I have established that the late Count Karlstein had no true title to the estate."

A gasp from everyone, then—except for me, for I'd heard it before, of course. But I hadn't expected this public announcement. Did they have something up their sleeves, this amazing pair? Miss Davenport was looking particularly smug. The audience was all ears, wide eyes, and open mouths, waiting for the next revelation.

"The true heir," said the lawyer, looking around in a way that made a courtroom of the village green and a learned judge of the Mayor, "was stolen from his cradle at birth, taken to Geneva, and abandoned. He was brought up in a foundlings' home, and then became a groom, and then a soldier, and fought Napoleon at the Battle of Bodelheim."

"Well, I'm blowed," said Max. "Who'd have thought it?"

"After the war," said the lawyer, "he became a coach-man, and then a humble servant—"

"What d'you think of that?" said Max, looking at Eliza. "Ain't that amazing? I wonder who he is?"

Meister Haifisch treated Max to a long cool look, as if to say, hold your tongue, my man, or I'll clear the court. Then he went on:

"The identity of this man is still in question. Fortunately, there is a certain way of telling. I have here"— he produced something, too small to see, from his waistcoat pocket and held it up—"the broken half of a silver coin, the other half of which was placed upon a chain and hung around his neck by the unhappy woman who stole him. She intended to hold him for ransom, but died before she could complete her plan. This coin"—he handed it to the Mayor, who peered at it closely—"and all the details, in her diary, were hidden away in an attic in Geneva and only recently found. So if the other half of the coin is traced—there is the new Count Karlstein!"

Something had been happening to Eliza in the last ten seconds or so—something that made her wriggle and thrust her hand down her neck and make little squeaking noises, as if a beetle had got down her dress. People were giving her very odd looks, but these changed to amazement when she held up a chain in the air and called:

"Here it is! He gave it to me! Didn't you, Maxie? Honest, Your Worship, sir! It was his! But he gave it to me as a token of his love, if you please, sir!" She ran to the platform, and then back again and caught Max's hand and dragged him forward, too.

"I've had that since I was a tiny baby!" he said. "Does that mean *I'm* Count Karlstein?"

The lawyer bent down and took the chain from Eliza's trembling hand. He and the Mayor held it up and compared it with the other. There was a pause of two or three seconds (and that's a mighty long time!) and then the Mayor nodded, and Meister Haifisch said:

"Yes, it does. The two halves match exactly! You are the one!"

Sensation…Hats flew in the air, and Eliza threw her arms around Max's neck, and the cheers were so loud that a flock of birds flew up in alarm from the trees across the green and added their squawking to the general tumult. As for Max, he didn't know where to put himself. He scratched his head, he beamed, he blushed, he dug his toes into the ground, he kissed Eliza, he blushed again, he grinned, he whistled, he winked at the Mayor's wife—and when the noise died away, he said:

"And all because of a plate of sausages…Well, thank you very much, Your Worship."

He bowed to the lawyer, who bowed back at him, very low, and said, "Not at all, Count Karlstein. I am delighted to be of service."

"Count Karlstein…" Max said it slowly, still unable to believe it. "But wait a minute. If I'm Count Karlstein, don't that mean that these girls is my relations, in a manner of speaking?"

"Most certainly," said Meister Haifisch, and he smiled at the two of them—sunshine; what a change in his dry old legal face!

"Then that's simple," said Max. "They don't have to go to an orphanage after all. They can live with me!"

Lucy and Charlotte ran to him in delight. He patted them on the head, unsure just yet of how an uncle should behave toward his nieces (but he'd soon learn), and then turned toward the person who'd been holding his hand.

"And I can marry Eliza!" he said, and kissed her to prove it.

And again, that might have been all—and the village would have a new lord and lady, and good ones, too: just and decent and popular—and we'd all have gone home rejoicing. But it wasn't quite over yet. For at that moment, Doctor Cadaverezzi came forward, with the chains still tightly around his wrists, and bowed very low—to Max, of course, as the lord.

"In view of the general happiness, your grace," he said courteously, "may one request an amnesty?"

And it was Miss Davenport who answered. She was taken aback—taken quite breathless, for a moment, and I don't suppose *that* had happened very often. She took a step backward, clasped her hands over her heart, and said:

"But—but this is…*Signor Rolipolio!*"

THREE

And he was, too.

And in spite of Max, who maintained that he was Doctor Cadaverezzi, and in spite of the sergeant, who said that, on the contrary, he was Luigi Brilliantini—and under arrest, what's more—it was Miss Davenport who had the last word on the subject.

"To me," she said firmly, glaring at the sergeant, "he will always be Rolipolio."

"Well," said Count Max Karlstein, "that settles it, I reckon, Sergeant. If he ain't Cadaverezzi and he ain't Brilliantini either, he can't have done whatever he did, can he? Stands to reason. You'll have to let him go."

"Count Karlstein," said Doctor Cadaverezzi, "you are too kind. But allow me…" He held his manacled hands in the air, gave them a little shake—and the chain came loose from his wrists and fell

240

ringing to the ground. He bowed, the audience clapped, and the sergeant gaped. "I was going to escape later on," explained Cadaverezzi-Brilliantini-Rolipolio, "but now I don't have to. Miss Davenport!" he said, turning to that lady and bowing very low before taking her hand, "I have been searching for you for many years—ever since our paths were separated long ago. And my good fortune is only equaled by my happiness, now that I have found you again!" And the two of them wandered away, talking very closely together. There was a gentle cough from Meister Haifisch. "Count Karlstein," he said, "there is a great deal to see to...."

Which is a good place to finish, I think. Because after that all the things that happened were simple things, ordinary, happy things, like marriages. And like the castle having a good spring-clean from top to bottom, and like me getting my job back. It was odd at first having Max as the master, and he found it odd, too, and there were times when he thought he wouldn't manage it. But common sense and fair play and good humor see you through most things, and he had a fund of those qualities. And Eliza, Countess Karlstein, was and is the perfect wife for a great lord.

Lucy and Charlotte went back to school. But not to any ordinary school—to a certain *Universal Academy of all the Arts and Sciences*, in Genoa, run by a Signora Rolipolio, a very learned lady, whose husband, the great actor Antonio Rolipolio, is the proprietor of the finest theater in all Italy. From time to time they made expeditions of scientific discovery to the pyramids, or to Mesopotamia, or to Hindoostan; and they insisted on taking me with them, and I went with great excitement, I can tell you. They spent all their holidays at Castle Karlstein, and over the years a kind of small miracle happened without anyone noticing it: they came to think of it as their home—that great, grim place, echoing with fear and dark with wickedness.

And soon I had some more children to look after, because Eliza and Max had a daughter, and then two sons, and then another daughter; and a rowdy lot they are, too. And then I married Wilhelm Bruchmann, a clockmaker, a great artist, and had children of my own, and Count Karlstein is their godfather.

It was Signora Rolipolio's idea to write the story of what happened, and she would have me do the bulk of it—but then, I suppose I saw more of it than anyone else. Sergeant Snitsch is an inspector now, and he searched out the police records to oblige Count Karlstein, and let us include his report of the night they arrested Doctor Cadaverezzi.

And that's all there is to tell. But still, on winter nights when the moon is high and the clouds race across it like a pack of hungry wolves, you can hear faint echoes of a hunting horn in the distant sky. And on All Souls' Eve every

house is shut, every door bolted—and every fireside is
ringed with wide-eyed faces, listening to the tales they tell
of the Prince of the Mountains, the Dark Hunter, the
Demon Zamiel.